'You'll all form pairs. For the first round, join hands with someone. The moment two people hold hands, you'll be considered a pair. The one person left without a partner will be disqualified.'

No one dared to ask what, exactly, *disqualified* meant.

PLEASE FORM PAIRS

First published in Great Britain in 2026 by Brazen, an imprint of
Octopus Publishing Group Ltd, Carmelite House
50 Victoria Embankment, London EC4Y 0DZ
www.octopusbooks.co.uk

An Hachette UK Company
www.hachette.co.uk

The authorized representative in the EEA is Hachette Ireland,
8 Castlecourt Centre, Dublin 15, D15 XTP3, Ireland (email: info@hbgi.ie)

First published in Japan in 2024 by Futabasha Publishers Ltd., Tokyo.
English translation rights arranged with Futabasha Publishers Ltd. through Emily Books Agency Ltd., Taiwan and Casanovas & Lynch Literary Agency, S.L.U., Spain.

This edition 2026.

Distributed in the US by Hachette Book Group,
1290 Avenue of the Americas, 4th and 5th Floors, New York, NY 10104

Distributed in Canada by Canadian Manda Group,
664 Annette St., Toronto, Ontario, Canada M6S 2C8

ISBN: 978-1-84601-753-7
eISBN: 978-1-84601-756-8

A CIP catalogue record for this book is available from the British Library.

Typeset in 10/14pt Farnham Text by Six Red Marbles UK, Thetford, Norfolk.

Printed and bound in Great Britain.

1 3 5 7 9 10 8 6 4 2

This FSC® label means that materials used for the product have been responsibly sourced.

MIX
Paper | Supporting responsible forestry
FSC® C104740
FSC
www.fsc.org

PLEASE FORM PAIRS

CHIREN KINA

TRANSLATED BY HAYDN TROWELL

brazen

The Classroom Hierarchy

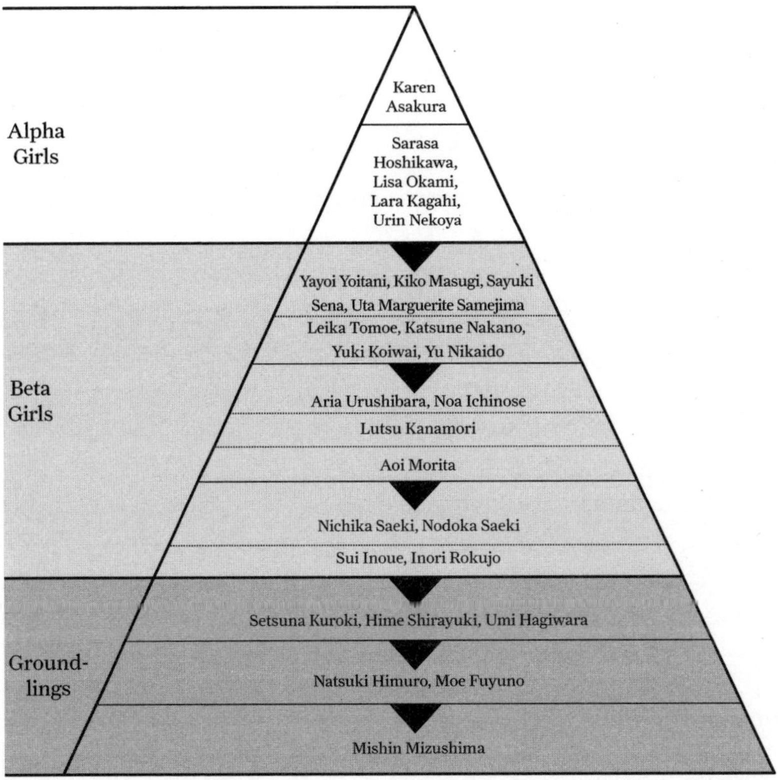

Prologue: The Classroom Hierarchy
Aria Urushibara

No day could be more depressing than when first-period gym class fell on a freezing winter morning.

Aria heaved a sigh from her corner of the classroom, where the icy air seemed to hang still, and watched as her breath turned a misty white.

As of January 2017, the high school she went to – said to be the oldest school building in all of Kyoto – wasn't equipped with air conditioning or heating in any of the classrooms.

Right across from Yasaka Shrine, in the heart of Gion where everything else was getting dressed up for tourists, this school alone stood out, like time had frozen before the war.

Aria had seen students posting pictures of the arched front entrance, the windows and the long, warm wooden hallways on Instagram, saying how *retro* it was.

If she had had the choice, she would have gone to the high school by the Kamo River, the one with the modern glass-panelled building she had visited during a mock exam in middle school. Her scores, however, were below average. Applying to that public school, where the smart kids went, would have been impossible in her position. The only option left was this private school – Yasaka Girls' High.

She pulled her gym clothes out of her *X-girl* tote bag – a magazine freebie – and glanced out the window.

Without her noticing it, snow had started falling. The gymnasium was bound to be even colder. Just thinking about it doubled her sense of despair. But no matter how much she hated it, gym class wasn't going anywhere.

Steeling herself, Aria stripped off her uniform like she was ripping off a band-aid, until she was down to her underwear. She had long since lost any sense of modesty that most high schoolers had. After all, this was an all-girls' school. Within six months of starting here, no one bothered to hide their underwear when changing, the way girls in co-ed schools would. Off to the side, one girl had even hopped up on the teacher's desk and was dancing in her underwear like a stripper.

That girl was Urin Nekoya – the class clown, and its biggest troublemaker.

Online, she went by *Urin*. Last summer, she uploaded a video to YouTube, a short clip called *A Boring Summer Day in the Life of a High School Girl*. Just as the title promised, it was about as plain as it got. But that video blew up, and all at once, she was popular.

At first, Aria couldn't stand her. But more than that, she felt like Urin was from a completely different planet.

Her bluish-black bob looked fake, almost like a wig. She always had powder-blue cat-ear headphones hanging around her neck and bright cobalt tights peeking out under her skirt. With a fashion sense that far out-there, there was no way Aria thought they could be friends.

And in truth, they *weren't* friends – just classmates. Nothing more, nothing less.

But curiosity got the better of her. She started watching Urin's videos, and her off-the-cuff way of talking soon became addictive. Aria found herself rooting for her – or at least, the version of her that lived on-screen. Just two days ago, during Urin's livestream to celebrate having reached one hundred thousand subscribers, Aria even left a 'Congrats!' message in the comments.

'Hey, Urin, you're going to get cancelled if someone spreads a clip of you like that.' Sitting at her desk in the middle of the room, Lisa Okami propped her chin on her hand and called lazily to Urin, still dancing in her underwear.

Lisa was a fan of Nicole Fujita and read *Popteen* religiously. She liked her eye makeup heavy, her skirt so short it was practically criminal and her hair dyed nearly blonde in clear violation of school rules. Teachers never said a word, though – probably because they had long since stopped expecting anything from a bottom-tier school like this, and partly because they were all plain scared of her. Aria was, too. Lisa was your classic *gyaru*, and intimidating as hell.

'Lisa-Lisa, my life ends when I die, okay? A little scandal won't kill my popularity. If anything, I'd love the extra clout. Actually, that's genius! Alright, everyone – go ahead and post my beautiful boobs!' Urin shouted to the room, squeezing together her snow-white chest.

'. . . You really are hopeless. And stop calling me Lisa-Lisa. It's so lame.'

Even as Lisa let out a sigh, she still snapped a picture on her phone, grinning at the ridiculous gravure poses Urin was striking.

Aria couldn't help but wonder what made people like them so different from her. Looking at Urin's porcelain skin, or the curves Lisa couldn't hide even under her gym clothes, the question gnawed at her.

Maybe it was genetics, maybe their upbringing. Whatever the reason, these so-called Alpha Girls had a certain sparkle. Just being spoken to by them was enough to make you shrink back in awe.

Compared to that, Aria had no aura whatsoever. Her skin was disappointingly healthy-looking, her chest was flat and she had just enough extra fat around her stomach to make her rush into her gym clothes, trying to cover it up.

'Oh, hey, Sarasa! Morning!' Urin, still in her underwear, waved at the girl entering the room from atop the teacher's desk.

Sarasa, of course, was another Alpha Girl.

'Um . . . What are you doing this early in the morning?' Sarasa Hoshikawa, starry-eyed but trying to play it off as exasperated, looked up at Urin.

'Urin's strip show!'

'. . . Right. Just get changed already. You'll catch a cold.'

'Idiots and geniuses don't get sick!'

'Which one are you supposed to be?'

Sarasa's perfectly tied ponytail swayed from side to side as she let out a bell-like laugh.

Aria pictured herself with the same hairstyle and cringed – it would definitely look bad on her. But on Sarasa, the very picture of purity, it was perfect.

Her eyes weren't huge, her nose wasn't sharp, her lips weren't full – and yet, if anyone asked, 'Who's the cutest in class?' every single one of them would answer Sarasa. Her beauty wasn't a copy of someone else's style, or something she forced by standing out. It was hers, and hers alone.

'Good morning, Aria,' Sarasa said, setting her bag on her desk.

Since the last seat shuffle had put them next to each other, she had greeted Aria like this every morning. Aria knew it didn't mean anything special, but that didn't stop it from lifting her mood ever so slightly.

'Morning. It's freezing today.'

'Yeah, it's so cold!'

'Hey, is that Burberry?' Aria asked, pointing at the beige-and-red check scarf Sarasa had just taken off.

'Yep. It used to be my sister's. She gave it to me.'

'Wow, it's so cute.'

'Thanks!'

Making an effort to keep her voice light and cheery, Aria felt – just for a second – that maybe she could be an Alpha Girl, too.

Sarasa wasn't as untouchable as Urin or Lisa, but still, Aria didn't want to push too close to her. She knew she wasn't fit to be *real* friends with her – and maybe, deep down, she accepted that. Chatting like this every now and then was enough for her.

Besides, she already had a best friend for life.

As long as that person was by her side, Aria could stand being hated by everyone else.

'Oh, Lara!'

No sooner did Sarasa take her seat than she lit up like a puppy spotting its owner and dashed toward the door. Coming in just before the bell was Lara Kagahi.

'Morning, Lara! Look at you, not late for once!'

That was the tone of voice Aria had wanted to hear – different from the one Sarasa had used with her.

'It was so cold I woke up early,' Lara yawned.

'Looking cool as always, Lara.'

'Even *with* the bedhead . . .'

A nearby student's comment left Aria nodding silently to herself.

Aria was definitely straight – she wanted a boyfriend as soon as possible – but she couldn't help but harbour a secret admiration for Lara. In fact, most girls at the school probably wanted to be noticed by her.

Because Lara was the school's *prince*.

She was tall – a hundred and seventy-five centimetres – and possessed sharp, androgynous features that made you forget she was a girl. She was already the ace of the basketball team, despite being a first-year. Normally, someone like that would get on the older students' nerves, but they adored her. During breaks, girls from other classes would literally show up calling out to her, screaming with excitement.

There was no way Aria could muster the guts to talk to her. A Beta Girl like her had no right to hog Lara's attention.

'Even if you're early, you're still barely on time. Anyway, hurry up and get changed – we have gym.'

'What, gym first period? Ugh . . . Sarasa, let's skip.'

'No way. You've already missed too many first periods. You'll fail.'

'True.'

Aria looked away and stood up. It wasn't jealousy. She wasn't really in love with her. Lara was just too dazzling to keep looking at for long – like staring straight into the sun from the bottom of a pool.

Needless to say, Lara was also an Alpha Girl.

In this class, the top tier was made up Urin, Lisa, Sarasa and Lara.

Within a month of starting first year, everyone knew where they stood in the classroom hierarchy.

At the very top were the Alpha Girls – the few per cent who

stood out, whether because they were pretty, brilliant at talking to people or just shone brighter than everyone else.

Then came the Beta Girls, the majority – too varied to lump under *ordinary*, but not exceptional, either.

Then, at the bottom, were the Groundlings – the ones considered unattractive, or else too strange to fit in.

Three broad layers, more or less.

Aria, average-looking and without any special talents, sat in the middle of the middle. She admired the top girls, of course, but she was oddly content where she was.

She wasn't glamorous like the Alpha Girls, but she wasn't stuck in the shadows like the Groundlings, either. She was just an average high schooler.

Besides, in all the stories popular among girls, the heroine was always just an ordinary girl.

And so, deep down, Aria believed that if some fateful event were to ever descend upon her classroom, it wouldn't come to any of them. It would come to her.

'Hey, Noa, are you ready? Let's go.'

Getting up from her seat, Aria called out to Noa Ichinose, like she always did. Unlike Aria's aisle seat by the hall, Noa's caught the sunlight by the window, something Aria couldn't help but envy.

'Yeah, I'm ready. Let's go.'

With a soft smile, Noa rose to her feet. *She* was Aria's best friend for life.

Naturally, Noa was a Beta Girl as well.

Maybe it was different at other schools, but here, best friends almost never crossed ranks. Which meant Noa was the same level as her – just another ordinary girl.

Still, Aria thought that if this school were co-ed, Noa would definitely get more attention from boys. Even Aria found her gentle aura soothing. There was something about her – a warm, enveloping presence – that left you feeling safe and secure.

'Cold today, huh?'

'Yeah, freezing.'

The icy January hallway felt like a march to the gallows.

Aria looped her arm through Noa's to fight off the chill.

The two of them had been together since elementary school. Living in the same neighbourhood meant walking to and from school together, and soon, they were hanging out at each other's houses after class. Noa's mum treated them like sisters, and every summer, her outdoorsy dad would take them camping.

In the forest, with the cries of animals echoing around them, the two of them would lie side by side in sleeping bags inside the tiny tent they pitched together. In those moments, Aria felt like she and Noa were the closest of sisters.

'What are we doing in gym today?' Aria asked, leaning into Noa for warmth.

'I think it's basketball.'

'Basketball, huh? I guess Lara will be showing off again.'

'For sure.'

Noa's Kyoto accent stretched out her words, turning her response into something like *Fawr shooore*. Lately, Aria felt like she had picked up a bit of it herself.

'We're lucky to be in the same class as her, huh?'

'For real.'

'Ah, I wish I had a boyfriend like her.'

'You'll have one soon, Aria.'

'You think so? But this is an all-girls' school. There aren't any guys around. It's hopeless.'

'Hopeless? You're so dramatic.'

Noa could laugh at the dumbest of things, which was why Aria always found herself more talkative whenever she was with her. Thanks to her presence, Aria felt like she could be the school's heroine despite her status as a Beta Girl.

'Alright, let's get started. Three laps around the gym,' called Norio Akiyama, their gym teacher, his half-hearted instructions echoing through the freezing gymnasium.

Shivering, Aria and the others began to run.

'God, Akiyama's so gross.'

'Right? I'd kill myself if he ever became my homeroom teacher.'

'At least we have someone else. She's kind of gloomy, but she doesn't nag much.'

'You mean Osuzu? She's probably just nervous because she's new.'

Even when she tried not to, Aria couldn't help but overhear Lisa and Urin griping as they ran ahead.

At a girls' school, male teachers – even old grandpas – were usually fawned over, but no one liked Akiyama.

Aria didn't, either. It wasn't like he had done anything to her personally, but there was nothing to like. The thick hair covering the backs of his hands, his clammy, greasy-looking skin – it was revolting.

'Alright, next, some warm-up stretches. Pair up however you want.'

No sooner had they finished running than he barked the next order, not even giving them a moment to catch their breath.

Behind her, Aria heard Lisa click her tongue. Akiyama's half-assed attitude and the way he treated students so carelessly were a big part of why everyone hated him.

'Let's pair up, Noa,' Aria said, reaching for her friend's hand.

'Yeah,' Noa answered, taking it without hesitation.

All around them, pairs were forming fast. Of course, everyone already knew who they would partner with before the order was given.

'You're left over again, Mizushima? Guess it's you and me today.'

Akiyama's tone – thoughtless and cruel – was probably half the reason he was so despised.

Mishin Mizushima nodded back in silence.

Having to pair up with Akiyama must have been hell.

Aria felt sorry for Mishin, but still, she turned her gaze away.

It was the same every time Akiyama gave that order. There were twenty-seven girls in the class, so one person was always left out – and no one was ever willing to step forward and pair with Mizushima, a ghostly Groundling sunk to the very bottom of the class.

Without thinking, Aria squeezed Noa's hand tighter.

'What's wrong?'

'Your hand's really warm.'

'Really?'

'Yeah,' she nodded, scanning the others out of the corner of her eye.

She was sure that, deep down, every girl here felt relieved – not that they would ever admit it. Thanks to Mizushima, they themselves were never the odd one out.

'Hey Noa, let's stay best friends forever, okay?'

Flashing her a smile, Aria tried to imagine who she would pair up with if she didn't have Noa. What if no one else offered to hold out a hand? What if she had to end up with Akiyama, like Mizushima? The thought was terrifying.

That was no exaggeration – Aria would rather die than end up isolated like that. At least, as long as she was still at high school.

Chapter 1: Please Form Pairs
Mishin Mizushima

Eight months into Mishin's second year of high school, around the end of autumn, a survey was handed out to everyone in class.

Survey on Bullying

This survey is being conducted so that all students can enjoy a positive, enriching school life. Your answers here will not be made public, and you don't have to write your name if you don't want to.

1. Do you feel that bullying is taking place at this school?

   Yes / No

2. Do you feel that you are being bullied right now?

   Yes / No

3. If you answered 'Yes', what form does the bullying take?

   ____

4. Do you feel that you are bullying someone right now, or that you have bullied someone in the past?

   Yes / No

5. If you answered 'Yes', what form does the bullying take?

   ____

6. What are your thoughts on bullying?

   ____

7. What do you think could be done to eliminate bullying?

   ____

'As you all know, two months ago, a student at an all-girls' high school in Tokyo tragically lost her life because of bullying over social media,' Asami Suzuta, their homeroom teacher again this year, said in her usual flat, unreadable tone. 'I can't help but feel deeply saddened every time I see the news. The survey I've just handed you is being conducted nationwide with the aim of eliminating bullying. As it says, you don't have to write your name if you don't want to, but please be sure to turn it in. Those who aren't on classroom-cleaning duty can go home after submitting it.'

Ms Suzuta had been in her first year of teaching when Mishin and her classmates started high school the year before. She looked young enough to pass for one of the students, a fact which earned her the nickname Osuzu among the Alpha and Beta Girls, who adored her. Needless to say, for someone like Mishin – a Groundling struggling for air at the very bottom of the third tier – it was impossible to call her something so familiar. To her, she was always *Ms Suzuta*.

She taught science, and though some students said her plain appearance and lack of expression made her the perfect picture of a no-frills science nerd, Mishin felt she carried herself with a certain intelligence. Not just outwardly, but inwardly, too. Unlike the self-righteous teachers who mistook bluster for justice, or the hopelessly oblivious ones, Ms Suzuta had consistently offered her genuine encouragement.

'If you're ever struggling with something, Mizushima, please tell me. I'll always be here to listen. I'm on your side, and anything you share will stay between us. Just remember that.'

She would say those words to her from time to time – quietly, without prying, after waiting to make sure there was no one else around.

Mishin had never mustered the will to actually confide in her. But just knowing someone cared was enough to ease, if only briefly, the vast loneliness pressing down on her.

2. Do you feel that you are being bullied right now?

Looking down at the paper with its blunt, unvarnished question – so different from Ms Suzuta's gentle encouragement – Mishin's body stiffened.

Yes / No

Those two were the only options.

She stared at the slash between *Yes* and *No*, her thoughts dragging her back through so many miserable memories.

Since entering high school, she could count on one hand the number of classmates who had spoken to her – and even then, only out of necessity, never for a casual chat. For two years in a row, she hadn't been invited to help with the culture festival. Whenever they had to pair off in gym class, she was always the one left over. And it wasn't just pitying looks she received – it was contempt, far too often for her to count. Every time those looks flashed back in her mind, the idea of going to school terrified her.

In those moments, Mishin would retreat into her imagination. What if, all of a sudden, everyone in class wanted to be her friend – would that erase this despair? She knew it was impossible, of course.

She wasn't even in the class group chat on LINE that the Alpha and Beta Girls were always gossiping about. She hadn't been invited. She didn't have any actual proof they were badmouthing her there, but she was all but certain they were.

She swallowed hard, a lump rising in her throat.

But I'm not *actually being bullied right now, am I?*

That thought only came to her because she had already lived through bullying in middle school – bullying so severe, both mentally and physically, that anyone could see it.

It started simply because, in gym class, she kept pairing up with another girl who was already being bullied.

As if passing the torch, that girl suddenly began ignoring her, and soon, the group chat filled with abusive messages on an almost daily basis. 'That ugly bitch has been getting full of herself lately.' 'When's she gonna drop out?' 'Stupid should go back to kindergarten.' They never named her, but everyone knew.

Her heart pounded to breaking with every notification – but looking back, that was still the easy part. She eventually left the chat, and no one attacked her directly after that. They only had power as a pack.

What hurt the most was finding foreign objects in her lunchbox – bugs, hair, trash.

'Please . . . I'm begging you, stop doing this! Apologize to my mum!'

The first time it happened, her anger boiled over and she raised her voice at the entire classroom. That only made it worse. The next day, the amount of garbage doubled.

But she couldn't throw away the lunches. Her clumsy mum had made them just for her, with everything she had. So, Mishin pushed the filth aside and forced herself to finish every bite, gagging as she went.

'I'm doing my best for you, Mishin, okay?'

Her mum's words echoed in her head as she chewed rice flecked with dust.

Her mum usually worked four nights a week, from evening until dawn, at a soapland in Kiyamachi. She was beautiful, but flighty – bad at school, never able to keep a normal job, falling for Gion hosts or being toyed with by worthless men who eventually spat insults at her and tossed her aside.

Her father must have been just as bad. Mishin barely remembered his face – he was gone by the time she was old enough to notice. The only thing that stood out was the memory of being hit when she was small.

By then, thoughts of death were always hovering in her mind. Every morning, she would arrive at school nauseous, bolting for the bathroom, wishing she could barricade herself there until the end of the day.

But she *couldn't* choose to escape, not while her mum was enduring hell, selling her body to support the two of them and pay her tuition. And since her mum was always home sleeping during school hours, she couldn't even pretend to be sick. Day after day, she dragged herself to class, knowing she was walking straight into more bullying.

The stress left its mark. In class, she started unconsciously pulling out her own hair, leaving bald patches that never grew back.

The memory of crawling insects in her lunch haunted her so badly that she couldn't eat at night. When her mum left a thousand-yen bill on the desk with a note telling her to buy herself something to eat, Mishin tucked it away in the cookie tin where she kept all her childhood treasures.

Her weight dropped rapidly. Each time she looked in the mirror, she thought she looked more and more like a ghost.

I'm a living ghost.

That was how she felt, right up until two days before the end of her second year of middle school.

On her desk, she found a slip of paper torn from a notebook, covered in neat handwriting:

> When's the funeral? The whole class is looking forward to attending.

The moment she read it, her soul seemed to drain out of her body. And at the same time, she felt strangely liberated. Maybe it was because she could finally believe with certainty that she was meant to die.

Ever since the bullying began, she had lost any sense of her own self-worth. And she couldn't bear the thought that her mum was putting herself through hell just so she could keep going to her own hell at school.

There were plenty of sleeping pills at home. Her mum took them practically every day.

Deciding it was time to end this miserable life of hers, Mishin went home.

That evening, the dining table was messier than usual. On it sat stacks of instant ramen, a bankbook with a cash card from the post office and a *My Melody* envelope.

Dear Mishin,

Happy birthday!

I remember when you were so small. I can hardly believe you're already fourteen. It feels like a dream.

Today, instead of a present, I have some happy news to share.

The truth is, I've fallen in love with someone. And he's fallen in love with me, too.

So, I'll be living with him for a while.

Forgive me for leaving so suddenly.

But don't worry. Once everything is settled, I'll come back for you. I'll work hard for that.

I'll keep sending money to the account, so make sure you eat properly, okay?

Even if we're apart, I'm always thinking of you, Mishin.

Love,

Mum

The message was written on cutesy *My Melody* stationery in pink pen, the round, bubbly letters like those of a high school girl.

After reading it carefully twice, Mishin folded the paper back into its envelope. She was laughing. She didn't even know why. Every feeling inside her had tangled together, like a broken toy.

She laughed until she was out of breath, as if her batteries had run down. Then, she pulled her empty lunchbox from her schoolbag and, without a moment's hesitation, tossed it into the trash.

From tomorrow on, she wouldn't have to choke down lunch while fighting the urge to vomit. She wouldn't have to bring lunch at all. If she got hungry, she could just buy bread at the school store.

Without dying, she had been released from hell. Both she and her mum.

Lying spread-eagle on the floor, where her mum's spilled Chanel perfume still lingered, Mishin drew in a deep breath. It felt like she was breathing properly for the first time in ages.

And so, in the run-down apartment her mum had left behind, Mishin began living alone.

Life was far more comfortable than before. She no longer had to tiptoe around. As long as she kept her attendance numbers in check, she could even skip school here and there.

Making excuses was a hassle, but other than being unable to attend the parent–teacher conferences, she wasn't inconvenienced. If she mailed the required forms to the address her mum had given – she had gone there once, to a shady-looking building where her mum clearly didn't live – they always came back properly filled out. Just as the letter had promised, money was deposited regularly.

And every year, without fail, on 17 March – her birthday – she received another letter. The handwriting never showed a hint of change, as though time itself had frozen.

She hadn't gone to her middle school graduation ceremony.

Her mum's letter had said, *I can't make it to your graduation. I'm sorry.* If nobody was going to congratulate her, then what was the point in going? Besides, she wanted to say goodbye to that classroom – a place that had always felt like her own funeral hall – as soon as possible.

To escape the bullying, Mishin hadn't taken the exam for the public high school most of her classmates attended. Instead, she enrolled at Yasaka Girls' High, a private school.

Part of her had still hoped she might make new friends. But with her ghost-like appearance, she knew it didn't matter what school she went to – she would end up on the very bottom rung. And she was right. Among the constant chatter in the classroom, her own voice was the only one missing. Once again, all she could do was pray not to become a target.

So now, in this class, to exist like a ghost wasn't the worst fate for her.

But still, was it really the right choice to circle *No* on that survey form?

What would her classmates write?

Through the curtain of bangs covering her eyes, Mishin looked at Lutsu Kanamori, who sat diagonally in front of her.

In the class's hierarchy, Lutsu ranked in the middle of the Beta Girls, but she was so smart it was a wonder she had ended up at this bottom-feeder of a school. Just this spring, she had even volunteered to be student council president.

Mishin also knew she was serious by nature, with a stronger sense of justice than most, whether inside the class or out.

Lutsu had gone to the same middle school as her. They had even shared a class in first and second year. Mishin still remembered that day, when Lutsu had spoken up against the bullying. But her sense of justice hadn't ended it. Like pouring oil on a fire, the malice had only flared up worse, until it was beyond saving.

That was why, afterward, Lutsu never spoke out against bullying again. Mishin understood – it couldn't be helped.

And yet, somewhere inside, she still carried the hope that Lutsu might one day save her.

That in gym class, she might choose her as a partner.

Despite knowing that was even less likely than being paired with one of the Alpha Girls.

After a while, Mishin turned in her completed survey and left the classroom.

She headed for the flowerbeds in the schoolyard.

The only time she ever truly felt glad to be alive was when she was tending flowers. The gardening club wasn't popular – she was its only member. But that was fine. In fact, being alone allowed her to relax.

She planted the new bulbs she had bought, recommended by the elderly florist she always went to.

'They'll bloom nicely,' he had told her.

Flowers are wonderful, she thought as she worked. *They're destined to be radiant from the moment they're born.*

Mishin wished that she could be a flower in her next life. Then, she wouldn't have to live so sorrowfully. Even three years later, the thorn of that day – being abandoned by her mum – was still lodged in her heart.

Her mum had been the one to name her. *Mishin*, written with the characters for *beautiful* and *heart*. 'So that you'll grow up with a beautiful heart,' she had said.

But Mishin already knew – there was no such thing as a beautiful heart.

She let out a deep breath, when a tennis ball bounced into the flowerbed.

Coming to fetch it was Sarasa Hoshikawa, captain of the tennis club and one of the Alpha Girls in Mishin's class. Without even glancing at her, Sarasa picked up the ball and walked off. Mishin went on planting her bulbs.

It wasn't that she had been ignored. Sarasa was at practice, and they weren't friends – there was no reason to talk.

Only after Sarasa's presence had completely faded did Mishin stop her hands and gaze at the flowerbed she had so carefully tended.

The flowers had bloomed so beautifully, and yet nobody ever noticed them.

Perhaps perspectives changed as you got older, but she had never once seen a student stop to admire them. Sarasa had been no different – ignoring not only her, but the flowers, too.

Beautiful people didn't necessarily have beautiful hearts. And even if they did, there was no rule that said they had to share that beauty with others. That was their choice. That was normal. It wasn't something to blame them for.

If I were Sarasa, I wouldn't talk to someone like me, either.

That was the simple truth.

And so, Mishin buried her welling sadness deep into the soil along with the bulbs.

The bulbs bloomed four months later, in February of the next year – 2018.

White flowers, drooping slightly as they opened. They looked like drops of snow turned into blossoms.

Mishin loved these flowers.

You can live beautifully even without looking up, they seemed to tell her.

'Hey, that flower's really pretty. Can you tell me what it's called?'

Startled, Mishin glanced up from the flowerbed.

Standing beside her, peering curiously at the flowers, was the cutest girl in the class.

'. . . Snowdrops,' Mishin answered after a moment, her eyes darting nervously, her heart pounding.

Yes – if anyone were to ask who the prettiest girl in the class was, everyone would have said Sarasa Hoshikawa.

At least, that was, before Karen Asakura transferred in.

'Snowdrops, huh? They *do* look like they're spun from snow.'

Karen crouched in front of the bed, nodding as she gazed at the newly opened flowers.

She had changed schools after moving from Tokyo near the end of last autumn, right around the time those surveys had been handed out.

'I'm Karen Asakura. Nice to meet you.'

The moment Karen appeared in her world, a scene from a novel Mishin once read flashed through her mind.

A breathtakingly pretty girl transfers from Tokyo into the class of an outcast girl stuck at the very bottom of the social hierarchy. The outcast, overwhelmed by the new girl's presence, imagines, *If a battle royale were to break out in this classroom, this girl would be the one to survive to the very end.*

Mishin had thought almost the exact same thing.

Karen's hair wasn't long and green like the heroine in that novel. It was a little past shoulder length, soft and fine, an ordinary reddish-brown. But no matter how plain her hairstyle, there was no question – Karen Asakura was chosen by the world.

How had the Alpha Girls felt, seeing her? When you're faced with someone undeniably more beautiful than yourself, do you feel admiration, or jealousy?

Mishin had no idea.

And she couldn't understand why this girl was talking to her, a Groundling stuck at the very bottom of the third tier.

'Do you like flowers, Mizushima?' Karen asked.

Mishin thought she was like a cat – no matter what she asked, no matter what she did, you could never dislike her. Her cuteness was something you could look at forever without growing tired.

Unable to meet her gaze, Mishin only nodded, head bowed like the snowdrops.

'Why do you like flowers?' Karen tilted her head, and a faint floral scent drifted from the tips of her swaying hair.

In the school's hierarchy, Karen was clearly an Alpha – yet she didn't belong to the other Alpha Girls' clique.

Instead, she had joined the student council – made up of Beta Girls closer to the third rank than the first, all serious types. Maybe the teachers had asked her to, since the girl she replaced on the council had transferred away just before she had transferred in. Karen even ate lunch with the other members.

The council here consisted only of a handful of people – Lutsu Kanamori as president, Karen Asakura and identical twin sisters, the older Nichika Saeki and the younger Nodoka Saeki. Because the school was small – just one class per grade, in a rough area of Gion with its nightlife and betting shops – the four of them were the only second-year members of the student council.

'. . . Because then I don't have to feel anything,' Mishin answered after a short pause.

She could never have confessed something so raw to anyone else in class. Maybe it was because, no matter the difference in rank, the others were all still human.

Karen, however, didn't feel like a fellow human at all. No matter how close she was, she seemed like someone on the other side of a TV screen, someone from another world altogether.

To Mishin, Karen was practically a god.

Why? Because in gym class, Karen chose to pair up with her instead of one of the other student council members.

Of course, it wasn't every time. Usually, Karen was paired with Lutsu, so when she partnered with Mishin, Lutsu would instead pair with the teacher, Akiyama. But to Mishin, those moments, once every two weeks, were priceless.

'I get it,' Karen said, still staring at the snowdrops.

Every time Karen spoke to her, Mishin felt as if her heart might leap out of her chest. She adored her that much.

And yet, inside, Mishin thought, *She'll never understand this kind of suffering. Unless she's reborn, there's no way she could know it. Because she's one of the chosen.*

'. . . I wish for your death,' Mishin murmured as she looked at the drooping blossoms.

'Huh?' Karen stared back at her in shock.

Of course she did. What Mishin just said was no different from suddenly telling her to die.

'Ah . . . It's the flower's meaning. Symbolically. The language of flowers,' she rushed to explain.

'Oh . . . The flower's meaning. You scared me,' Karen laughed, her smile returning as if she had come back to life.

'I'm sorry.'

As she apologized, Mishin's heart churned. Why had she spoken such a violent phrase to her own goddess? It felt like some cruel message from her past had suddenly come loose and fallen onto her.

'So, why did you decide to plant these? Do you want someone to die?'

Mishin's breath caught in her throat.

No one had ever asked her something so blunt. And never in her wildest dreams had she imagined such a question could come from the lips of someone as delicate and lovely as Karen.

. . . Someone she wished dead.

Faces of the classmates who had bullied her flickered through her mind – along with one face in particular.

'I just like them . . . That's all,' Mishin answered, stroking the petals gently.

Yes, that was the only response she could bring herself to give.

'I see. Well, I like them too now,' Karen said warmly.

With that smile, directed at her alone, flowers seemed to burst into bloom all through Mishin's chest.

The snowdrops bloomed again a year later, in mid-February of 2019, just a month before graduation.

'I wish for your death.'

The voice came from behind her. When Mishin turned around, she spotted Karen standing there. Her reddish-brown hair was a little lighter than last year, grown out from shoulder-length to fall neatly past her shoulders.

'The snowdrops bloomed again, huh? I thought their meaning was so creepy when you told me about them last year. There's no way I could forget.' Karen smiled, squatting in front of the flowerbed.

Mishin nodded, savouring the joy of hearing Karen talk to her again after several days of silence.

Her final year of high school had passed without change – she was still a living ghost. She never joined in with the classroom circle, breathing instead at the very bottom of the social hierarchy. By this time of year, even at a bottom-tier school like this one, everyone was too wrapped up in their own plans for the future to bother singling her out. It wasn't so much that she was being ignored anymore – she was simply invisible to them now.

In the end, her high school years contained nothing that could be called *the joy of youth*. Still, on days like this – when she could talk with Karen, when their eyes met across the classroom or when she paired up with her – Mishin could feel, just for a moment, like she was functioning as an ordinary high school girl.

'Hey, did you plant something new here?' Karen ran her fingers over the freshly planted seedlings, unbothered by the dirt.

Mishin nodded again. The rose saplings had been another recommendation from the old man at her favourite flower shop.

'But graduation's coming up. Who's going to take care of it?'

Karen's question, innocent as it was, caused Mishin to freeze up.

She was right . . . Somehow, Mishin had felt like this flowerbed would be hers forever. She had planted something new here even though there was no guarantee new members would join the club, no certainty anyone would tend to them after she was gone. All at once, planting fresh flowers felt like a crime.

'I . . . hadn't thought about that . . .' she answered, blaming herself for being so thoughtless.

Sometimes, she found herself speaking a little too formally with Karen, even though they were the same age. Maybe it was because she admired her. Or maybe, by now, Mishin simply couldn't remember how she was supposed to speak with classmates.

'I figured,' Karen laughed. 'So, what are you going do after graduation?'

'. . . I'm planning to work part-time.'

Most of the students in her class would probably go on to college or vocational school. Mishin wasn't without a longing for campus life herself, but after losing her communication skills over the past few years, she couldn't picture herself enjoying it. Besides, she had a quiet dream of her own.

'At my favourite florist,' she added softly, imagining herself bringing that vision to life.

It was the same shop where she had bought the snowdrops and rose saplings, and the kindly owner had agreed to hire her mostly out of goodwill.

When she had asked to work there, it had felt like leaping from the balcony at Kiyomizu Temple. But the old man had said, 'You're in luck. I've been needing some help. I can't afford to hire a full-time employee, though. Would part-time be alright?'

Mishin had nodded twice, hard. No matter how low the pay, she had always dreamed of working with him, in that shop brimming with love for flowers.

'A florist, huh? That sounds nice.'

Karen's upbeat response filled Mishin with joy, and she nodded eagerly.

She wanted to be independent – to earn enough to live modestly, and to survive on her own.

'. . . It's my dream to open a small flower shop of my own one day.'

And someday, to make that dream real.

'Wow. You already have a dream. That's wonderful, Mizushima.'

Karen's smile lit the air like spring sunlight streaming into a room whose curtains had been shut for years.

'Yeah.'

Her voice trembled with excitement.

She had loved flowers since she was a child. When she was ten, her mum had asked what she wanted to be when she grew up, and Mishin had answered, 'A florist.'

But her mum's response had shattered that dream.

'Oh, come on. What *is* that? That's too boring. You might not get it yet, but being a florist is not at all the star of the show, you know? It's not all sparkly and pretty like you think. It's early mornings, hard work and kind of dirty. Plus, you'd barely make anything at all. Come on, don't you want to be something else? Something that actually pays? Something proper?'

Looking back, her mum's favourite word had always been *proper*.

Mishin had sensed there must be some grudge behind that dismissal. Never before had she been rejected so harshly.

Before working at a soapland, her mum had been a hostess at a Gion bar. She had probably seen florists come decorate the place or deliver bouquets for birthdays and events – and from that, decided they were second-rate.

But Mishin realized something – no one had ever sent flowers to her mum.

From then on, she had locked her dream away inside her chest, never telling anyone. She couldn't bear to have it denied and defiled. But just now, telling Karen hadn't been hard at all. She had even wanted to say it.

'When you open it, I'll come buy a bouquet.'

Maybe she had told her because she hoped Karen would respond like this – with gentle words that sprinkled light onto her dream.

'What about you, Asakura? What will you do after graduation?' Mishin asked.

For the first time in a long while, she felt colour stir inside her.

'I'm going back to Tokyo. I got into a good university thanks to Lutsu tutoring me. Miracle, right? I mean, being in the student council when you're as dumb as me? Kind of funny, don't you think?'

It was true Karen wasn't a star student. Mishin had seen her attending make-up classes and retests more than once.

'By the way, Lutsu says she wants to be a teacher,' Karen went on. 'Isn't that amazing? I really admire her.'

. . . Lutsu. The name made Mishin's chest tighten.

Karen and Lutsu had grown close enough this past year to be called best friends. Even watching from the sidelines of their classroom, Mishin didn't have a shred of doubt about it.

Maybe because she was a natural honours student, Lutsu had always looked the part – glasses, neat shoulder-length black hair tucked precisely behind her ears, freckles across her cheeks like Anne of Green Gables. Honestly, she didn't look like a match at all next to Karen, who was stunningly pretty. But appearances were only surface-level.

People were always drawn to those who had what they themselves lacked.

That was why Mishin loved flowers, and why Karen dazzled her – because Karen had everything she didn't. And surely, Karen felt the same way about Lutsu.

Some students frowned at the mismatch between the glamorous Karen and the plain Lutsu, but Mishin understood. Karen wasn't the kind of person who cared about the school hierarchy. If she were, she would never have partnered with someone from the very bottom. And no matter who she befriended, her own rank would never drop.

Still, if Lutsu was aiming to become a teacher, she should have been able to get into a higher-level school. Like that famous public high school by the Kamo River, the one everyone dreamed of.

In that case, why had she chosen this bottom-tier girls' school?

And when had she first started dreaming of becoming a teacher?

'. . . Asakura? Why did you transfer here, anyway?' Mishin asked, remembering the day she had first spoken to Lutsu.

'Well . . . I stopped going to school for a while.'

The answer was nothing like what she had expected.

Lutsu would probably have asked why, innocently, without hesitation. Maybe Karen had even wanted her to ask. But Mishin didn't have the courage.

While she was still searching for words, the bell rang.

'See you at graduation! Let's take a picture, okay?'

Karen stood, skirt swishing, and walked off, showing no sign of regret over the abrupt end to the conversation.

Watching her disappear from sight, Mishin let out a long sigh.

If only she were as beautiful as Karen. If only she were as smart as Lutsu. Maybe then, she could have been Karen's friend, openly and honestly, the two of them calling each other by their first names.

Just once, she wished Karen would address her as a friend.

But that would never happen now.

After graduation, she would never see her again. Especially not once she left for Tokyo.

Even best friends couldn't stay together forever.

Friendship was fragile. More fleeting than anything else. That was what Mishin believed.

Dear Mishin,

Happy birthday.

And congratulations on graduating high school.

You did really well, getting through those three years on your own.

I'm sorry I couldn't come to see you, or do anything to help you.

But Mishin, there hasn't been a single day since then that I've forgotten you.

If nothing else, please believe that.

And! I'll be at your graduation tomorrow. I even went all out and bought a suit for the occasion.

After the ceremony, let's talk properly about your future.

Once Mishin finished reading the letter she had pulled from the mailbox, she folded it up and slipped it into the breast pocket of her blazer. She had known it had arrived yesterday, but hadn't dared open it until this morning. She had been too scared to read it. If it had said again, 'I can't come to your graduation,' she knew she wouldn't have been able to get out of bed.

Turning the corner by the house with the white plum blossoms, she quickened her pace toward school, her steps driven by the excitement of finally seeing her mum again after four long years.

This would be the last time she passed through these gates.

When she arrived, she looked up at the faded old building, feeling a twinge of something like wistfulness. She had always hated school, but she liked this classical-looking building that stood tall in the middle of the bustling downtown area.

Because the grounds were so small, the gymnasium – also used as the auditorium – was no larger than a basketball court. So, as always, only the third-year students would attend graduation.

She walked down the deserted hallway and slipped silently into the classroom. On each desk sat a corsage – a bright yellow rose with a tag reading *Congratulations on Graduating!* – with some students already having pinned theirs to their chests.

Mishin took her seat in the centre of the back row and, like the others, fastened the corsage to the pocket on the left breast of her uniform.

The room was strangely restless.

It wasn't the sad, heavy atmosphere of friends parting ways.

The voices flying back and forth were closer to anger, or confusion.

Her eyesight wasn't great, so it took Mishin a while to notice what was causing the commotion. She hadn't even realized that the farewell messages they had scrawled on the blackboard after their last February class had been wiped away. That was because she herself hadn't written anything on it.

But as she listened carefully to her classmates' voices, she finally caught on, her eyes narrowing as she took in the blackboard. She didn't know what had been written there before, but something about the words now written in white chalk against the green board felt wrong.

The handwriting was unmistakably that of their homeroom teacher, Ms Suzuta. But instead of the usual encouraging message from a teacher to her graduating students, what was written looked more like the rules of some sort of game.

Special Lesson

- Please form pairs.
- The moment you take someone's hand, you will be officially paired with them.
- Anyone who cannot pair up will be disqualified.
- Once everyone is paired and the disqualified person for that round is determined, the game will proceed to the next round.
- You cannot pair with the same person twice.
- If the remaining number is even, one person must sit out. The person to sit out will be decided by vote.
- Once the number of participants drops below half, every round must begin with the call, 'Please form pairs.' If this rule is broken, the round will be void.
- If the **designated student** is purposefully excluded by the others, then everyone except that student will be disqualified.
- The last one or two remaining will be permitted to graduate. Graduates must not be late to the ceremony.
- The lesson will last for sixty minutes.
- If no graduates are decided before the ceremony, everyone will be disqualified.

Notes

- Anyone who leaves the classroom during the lesson will be disqualified immediately.
- Anyone who removes their corsage will be disqualified. Anyone whose corsage is removed by another student will also be disqualified.

'What the hell's this *special lesson* supposed to be?'

'*Please form pairs*? Is this gym class or something?'

'And what's with all that *disqualified* stuff?'

'Does that mean if you're disqualified, you can't go to graduation?'

'No way, that's crazy.'

Maybe because school rules were about to stop applying, Lisa Okami, now with bleached blonde hair, and Urin Nekoya, who had clearly had some work done on her eyelids over spring break, were cracking jokes about the strange rules written on the board. Mishin had never once spoken with either of these Alpha Girls, nor had she ever felt the urge to.

But staring at the blackboard, she felt a cold dread spreading through her body.

'Morning!'

Before long, Lara Kagahi – the so-called prince of their all-girls high school since the day she enrolled – sauntered in, sounding as sleepy as ever.

'Morning, Lara. You're cutting it close on graduation day, huh?' Sarasa, ponytail swinging and the tag of her corsage fluttering, rushed straight toward her. 'Hey, Lara, look at this. Someone rubbed out the farewell messages we all wrote on the blackboard and wrote these creepy rules instead.'

Sarasa's voice dripped with sweetness as she spoke to Lara, so unlike the girl Mishin remembered bending to retrieve a stray tennis ball near the flowerbeds. Even on the last day of school, the Alpha Girls clung to their cliques and favouritism as if nothing had changed. Mishin felt a quiet disappointment settle in.

'For real. What's this about pairing up . . .?' Lara mumbled, still rubbing sleep from her eyes.

It was at that moment that their homeroom teacher of three years, Asami Suzuta, entered the classroom.

'Hey, Osuzu! What's this?' Urin mumbled, pointing at the blackboard.

Normally, Ms Suzuta would answer even the silliest student question, but today, she ignored Urin and stepped up to the podium. Probably because it was graduation day, she wasn't wearing her usual slacks, but rather a jet-black skirt suit that looked almost like mourning clothes. Against that black, pinned to her collar, she wore the same yellow rose corsage the students had, almost unnervingly bright.

'Good morning, everyone. And congratulations on reaching this special day.'

A shiver ran down Mishin's spine. Ms Suzuta, famous among the students for being so expressionless, was smiling with a radiance she had never shown before. She looked like she had been waiting for this day with all her heart, like nothing would make her happier than seeing her students graduate.

'Come on, Osuzu, enough with the formal stuff. What's this written on the board?' Urin cut in again.

But Ms Suzuta continued to ignore her. 'Today's the day of your graduation ceremony. But before that, I'd like us to have one final lesson together.'

Urin threw her hands up at neck height, pulling a comical face at the students behind her as if to say, *Can you believe this?*

'This will be a very special lesson, one only selected students get to experience – and one you'll never forget.'

Her eyes seemed fixed on a scroll taped to the back wall – on it, *Hope* was written in bold characters by the calligraphy club.

'Yeah, but what's that actually supposed to mean?' Urin snapped.

Her desk was right in front of the teacher's, so there was no way she hadn't heard her. And yet, Ms Suzuta went on speaking without so much as glancing her way.

'Yes. Congratulations, everyone. Our class has been selected to take part in the *Voices Against Bullying* campaign.'

Congratulations, she repeated, in a cheerful tone completely at odds with the teacher they knew, smiling as she broke out into a solitary applause. The strangeness of it all had Mishin catching her breath. The classroom's once-lively buzz dulled into an uneasy murmur.

'Uh . . . Don't you think Osuzu's acting weird today?'

'Yeah. Really weird . . .'

The students in the front row started whispering to themselves, no doubt thinking the same thing.

For three years, Ms Suzuta had been well-liked by her students – or to put it another way, they hadn't taken her seriously. The small age gap helped, but so did her gloomy atmosphere that skirted the edge of cool, not to mention she was so timid that, despite being their homeroom teacher, she hadn't once called Lisa out for dyeing her hair against school rules.

'Now then. The instructions on the board are part of this campaign. But before I explain, do you all remember the survey we handed out in the fall of your second year? The one about bullying? The results of that survey tell us that this class has a bullying problem. That's something that should never have been tolerated. Some of you even wrote that bullies deserve the death penalty. For three years now, I've felt the exact same way.'

She ploughed ahead, leaving them no chance to interrupt. This was a completely different woman from the teacher who usually clammed up when teased, a fiery resolve radiating from within her.

Nobody had the faintest idea what this *special lesson* could be. With a title like *Voices Against Bullying*, maybe it was going to be some justice-driven activity? But the only thing written on the board was *Please form pairs* – a phrase so traumatic it made Mishin's chest pound. Every cell in her body screamed at her to get out of the room.

'What? There's no bullying here,' Lisa said, her voice clipped.

Mishin's fingertips trembled.

Of course. Being ignored, never having anyone partner with her, knowing her classmates were gossiping about her in the LINE group chat – those weren't bullying. At least, not to anyone but her.

'Maybe you remember – several months before that survey, a student in Tokyo killed herself after being bullied on social media.

The bullies were never arrested. They faced no punishment. They went on with their lives, looking forward to their futures. They forgot what they'd done and grew up. One day, they'll have kids of their own who will go on bullying. At this rate, it will never be eradicated. And the kind of invisible bullying that went on in this classroom will never disappear.' Ms Suzuta's words spilled out fast, almost violently polite, her voice rising and falling with each breath.

'Uh . . . I seriously don't get it. What are you even *saying* all of a sudden? Are you feeling okay?' Lisa quipped, her long, toned legs shifting restlessly under her desk like they were voicing her anger at being ignored.

That was when Ms Suzuta suddenly smiled. 'Lisa Okami. You're right, aren't you? It doesn't make sense. Maybe there really isn't any bullying in this class. Maybe it was all in someone's imagination. Maybe the student who felt bullied was just being oversensitive. I couldn't do anything about invisible bullying, either. But that's exactly why, through this special lesson, I want you all to think about it. For example – how it feels when the gym teacher says *Partner up*, and you're the only one left out.'

Nobody looked at her directly, but Mishin could feel every gaze in the room suddenly burn into her skin.

'Morning.'

It was the gym teacher, Mr Akiyama, strolling in with a typical half-dead greeting just as the classroom fell silent.

The hair sprouting from the hands poking from his suit sleeves hit Mishin's vision like a slap. She didn't hate Mr Akiyama – he was the only one who ever partnered with her – but that wiry hair always made her stomach turn. It reminded her of finding something nasty in her lunch.

'Suzuta? What's this about? I'm supposed to be getting ready for the ceremony,' Mr Akiyama demanded, visibly irritated.

Ms Suzuta must have called him in. Turning toward the door, she fixed him with a glare full of loathing and spite. 'One of the survey responses also said this: *It would be good if no one student always ended up partnered with the teacher in gym class.*'

At that, Mishin's heart nearly stopped.

She wanted to stand up, to bolt from her seat, but her body was frozen stiff. Because the one who had written those words on the survey was she herself.

'. . . What are you talking about, Suzuta?' Mr Akiyama glared back.

'Forgive me, but you always knew one student would be left over in gym. And yet, for three years, you kept making them form pairs on their own, didn't you? Even though I specifically asked you to sometimes pair them up in roll-call order.'

Ms Suzuta spoke in a rapid-fire torrent, her tone so unlike her usual self that even Mr Akiyama was left standing there, mouth agape.

'Uh . . . Suzuta?' he began at last. 'What's this all of a sudden? I don't really follow. In every school I know, students make pairs for warm-ups in gym class. That's just how it is. And this class has an odd number of students. Even if I go by roll-call order, *someone's* going to be left out. So, I let them team up with their friends. I'm just trying to be considerate,' he said with a sheepish grin.

Ms Suzuta let out a long, despairing sigh.

'Have you ever stopped to think how it feels to be the student who's always left out?'

This time, Mr Akiyama heaved a sigh of his own. 'That's not our concern as teachers, is it?'

Ms Suzuta turned to face the students, putting her hands together with a loud clap. 'Alright. I'm sure by now you all feel the same way I do. Yes? Needless to say, what Mr Akiyama has been doing to that student amounts to bullying. Therefore, I've decided that he will be joining our special lesson today.'

Once more, the sound of solitary applause echoed through the classroom.

Then, with a calm smile, Ms Suzuta slipped the yellow rose

corsage from her own lapel and, without hesitation, pinned it to Mr Akiyama's suit jacket.

'Um . . . What are you doing? And what's this about a special lesson? Look, like I said, I'm really busy right now. Of all days, all the other teachers decided to show up late. I can't get through to anyone. And it's graduation day! Unbelievable. Once you're done with homeroom, come help me, would you? I can't even find the key to the supply room in the basement to get the red-and-white curtains. I'm really in a bind here. We need everything set up before the parents arrive, never mind the students . . .' Mr Akiyama muttered in exasperation.

Then, as if to say he had had enough, he turned on his heel. He didn't bother to remove the corsage pinned awkwardly to his chest – too much trouble, probably.

'Class has already started, Mr Akiyama. Did you read the rules on the blackboard? Leave the room, and you'll be disqualified,' called Ms Suzuta, her voice stabbing at his back.

Mishin squinted again at the blackboard.

- Anyone who leaves the classroom during the lesson will be disqualified immediately.

Just as Ms Suzuta said, that was apparently one of the rules.

But what the rules referred to, and what exactly *disqualified* meant, Mishin had no idea. No one had explained.

Mr Akiyama heaved another sigh, louder this time. 'Fine. Disqualified or whatever, I'm leaving.'

He tossed the words over his shoulder and stepped into the hallway without so much as a glance at the rules on the board.

That was when the downpour began.

Mishin instinctively turned toward the window. Rain was coming down heavily, like it was trying to wash away the filth of the world.

'Ugh, gross!' Urin's voice rang out over the pounding rain.

When Mishin turned to look, Mr Akiyama was swaying unsteadily in the doorway between the classroom and the hall, like some kind of zombie. The next instant, his eyes rolled upward, and that broad, heavy back she had seen so many times before seemed to be sucked down toward the classroom floor as he collapsed with a loud thud.

Several students in the front row – including Urin – shrieked.

'Everyone, please be quiet. I'm afraid I have some bad news. Mr Akiyama has been disqualified,' Ms Suzuta declared in a flat voice.

Disqualified.

Mishin still couldn't grasp what the word meant.

From the doorway where he had fallen, Mr Akiyama's upturned face happened to be staring into the skirt of Nodoka Saeki, the younger of the Saeki twins, who sat in the front row by the corridor.

Nodoka raised her hand slightly, her voice trembling. 'Um . . . Ms Suzuta? Mr Akiyama isn't moving . . .'

Indeed, the gym teacher showed no sign of getting up.

Right after her sister spoke, her twin, Nichika, seated immediately behind her, stood up to check on him.

'. . . Wait, is there, like, a chance he's actually dead?'

The one who chirped that out wasn't Nichika, but Urin, leaning over her desk to get a better look.

As if to test that theory, Nichika slowly reached toward Mr Akiyama's mouth to see if he was still breathing. But before she could, Ms Suzuta grabbed her wrist. 'Sit down, Nichika Saeki,' she said in an uncharacteristically sharp tone. 'You too, Urin Nekoya. I'm about to explain the special lesson.'

It was Lisa who finally broke, fed up with Ms Suzuta's sudden shift into authoritarianism. 'Look, whatever this *special lesson* or *anti-bullying campaign* crap is supposed to be, there's no bullying in this class, so quit with the personality flip and stop acting like you suddenly own the place. And seriously, what the hell does *disqualified* even mean? Why did Akiyama just keel over?'

Lisa's tone and language were as awful as always, but she was voicing the exact same questions every single one of them wanted answered.

Ms Suzuta let go of Nichika's arm, went back to the podium,

and slowly faced the back of the room. Mishin realized she was once more staring at the word on the calligraphy scroll on the back wall – *Hope*.

'You really don't see it, do you? You can't see what's been happening right here in this very classroom. Very well. Then let me tell you a story . . . This all happened back when I was a high schooler, just like all of you.' With a cold little smile, as though a stage curtain were rising, she began. 'There was bullying in my class. But not everyone was aware of it. Some people could see the student being bullied, others couldn't. The teachers who didn't see it went on like nothing was wrong. In gym class, for instance, they'd say, *Pair up with someone*, not realizing that for me, that was basically torture . . . Yes. I was always the one left over. Not a single classmate would ever pair up with me. But it wasn't like they consciously left me out – they just picked their close friends first. And me – I was the class ghost. I knew they called me that behind my back. My drab looks and gloomy personality – I understood that was why. Still, every time I was left out, I wanted to die. To sit there, stabbed by loneliness in the middle of everyone else's cheerful chatter, forced to keep being a ghost – it was unbearable. But nobody had any idea how I felt. Which meant there wasn't really any *bullying*. To everyone else, it was just everyday life.'

Of course, seven years ago, Ms Suzuta had been a student like them. To Mishin, the scenes she was describing were vividly seared into her imagination.

'But then, one day near graduation, my school was chosen to run the *Voices Against Bullying* campaign. And as part of the *special lesson* that came with it, we played a certain game. Through that game, every one of my classmates came to realize that they had been excluding me, that inside them all was an *unconscious malice*. I was so happy . . . For the first time in my life, I felt hope. I felt like justice really did exist. I pray that someday, bullying will truly disappear from this world. That no student will have to feel the way I did.'

By the time her speech-like confession came to an end, the classroom had fallen completely still.

Mishin exhaled slowly, deliberately. She realized she had stopped breathing as she listened, as though possessed by Ms Suzuta's high-school self.

'And so . . .'

A sharp clap of her hands rang out over the sound of rain hammering the classroom.

Facing her stunned students, Ms Suzuta declared loudly, 'Starting now, you're all going to take part in the exact same graduation game I once did.'

Game?

The way she said it carried none of the warmth usually attached to that word.

'I'm sorry for keeping you waiting on your question, Urin Nekoya. Now, let me explain the rules I wrote on the board properly. I'll only say this once, so watch the board and listen carefully.'

Her voice had returned to its usual blank but gentle tone. She *had* heard Urin, after all. Mishin felt her heart pounding faster as she looked at the blackboard. The rain hitting the windows was growing increasingly heavy.

'You'll all form pairs. For the first round, join hands with someone. The moment two people hold hands, you'll be considered a pair. The one person left without a partner will be disqualified.'

No one dared to ask what, exactly, *disqualified* meant.

Mr Akiyama, who had been disqualified for leaving the room, still lay as motionless as a corpse.

But someone that big couldn't die from a mere fall – he was no doubt just unconscious. At least, Mishin told herself that. The others must have been trying to convince themselves of the same thing.

'With Mr Akiyama gone, there are now twenty-seven of you. So, in the second round, it will start with twenty-six. Since that's an even number, no one will be left over. Instead, you'll first vote on one person who will sit out. How you vote is up to you. Once that person is chosen, the remaining twenty-five will pair up again. Just like the first round, the individual left out will be disqualified. Be careful – if you pair with the same person twice, that will result in a disqualification. You'll keep going on like this until there are only one or two of you left. Simple, don't you think?' Ms Suzuta chuckled as if shaking off an evil spirit. 'Follow the detailed rules written on the board. Since we're short on staff, I'll go prepare for the graduation ceremony. It will start at ten o'clock, exactly one hour from now. Whoever is left standing by then, don't be late.'

As their homeroom teacher stepped down from the podium, Mishin couldn't fail to notice her hand trembling slightly.

'I'll take care of this,' Ms Suzuta said lightly, almost casually, as she grabbed Mr Akiyama's ankles where he lay at Nodoka's feet and dragged him out into the hall.

For several long seconds, only that sound and the pouring rain echoed in the classroom.

'. . . So, basically . . . could this be one of those death games?'

It was Urin who spoke up half in jest, her voice strangely buoyant, like she was actually enjoying the situation.

'No way. This game crap is so *lame*. I'm not doing it,' Lisa snorted, reaching for the phone she had left in plain sight on her desk. On the brightly lit lock screen, Nicole Fujita flashed a cute smile, making a peace sign by her lips. Yet her own smile vanished almost immediately.

'What? No service?'

Lisa slammed her phone down face-first on the desk, crushing the image of the fashion model.

Even though Ms Suzuta was gone, Mishin quietly checked her own phone under her desk. It similarly showed no signal.

'Wait, me too!'

'Same here.'

'What the hell? This sucks.'

'So, what even is this game?'

'Beats me.'

'What about Akiyama?'

'This is freaking me out.'

'I need to go to the bathroom.'

'But if we leave the room, we're disqualified . . .'

'What do we do?'

'I don't know.'

'Ugh, I can't even reply to my boyfriend!'

'For real.'

The tension must have finally snapped, as everyone started chattering at once. It seemed none of their phones had service anymore. They had all been working fine until Ms Suzuta left, so maybe she had activated some kind of signal jammer. But as far as anyone could see, there was no sign of any such device in the room.

Still, Mishin wasn't as rattled by the lack of reception as the others. Her phone had been cut off six months after her mum left – it always read *No Service*. She only kept it to tell the time and to connect to Wi-Fi hotspots.

Cautiously, she glanced to the seat at her right – to Karen Asakura, who had ended up seated beside her in the last shuffle.

Unlike the others, Karen hadn't taken out her phone at all. Her face looked utterly normal, to a startling degree. Mishin couldn't help staring at that beautiful, faintly childish face. There wasn't a trace of fear about her – if anything, her eyes let off a defiant glint, as if deep down, she might even be excited.

Next, Mishin slowly looked left.

Her other new neighbour from the last seat change, Lutsu Kanamori, was sitting perfectly upright, eyes fixed on the blackboard, like she thought class was about to start as usual. Unlike Karen, however, her face was stiff with fear.

Maybe she felt Mishin's gaze, because she almost looked back. Panicking, Mishin hurried to turn away.

'Calm down, Nodoka. It's okay. It's okay,' came Nichika's voice from the front.

Mishin looked over. Nodoka had collapsed on the floor, pale and gasping, while Nichika was rubbing her back, trying to soothe her.

'Hey, you two – you got a good look at him, right? What happened to Akiyama?' Lisa, sitting in the middle of the classroom, called to the Saeki twins, her irritation at the lack of phone reception spilling over into her voice.

The only ones who had clearly seen Akiyama's condition when he was disqualified were Nodoka, sitting in the very front row by the hall, and her twin behind her, Nichika. Everyone wanted to know, of course. But pressing a girl who was on the verge of hyperventilating for an answer felt needlessly cruel.

'Hey, are you listening? He wasn't dead or anything, was he?' Lisa pressed without a shred of concern.

Already breathing erratically, Nodoka tipped into full hyperventilation.

Jumping to her feet, Nichika pulled a plastic bag from her schoolbag and held it to her sister's mouth. Mishin had never seen Nodoka like this in class before, but the practised way Nichika handled it made it clear this wasn't the first time.

'I didn't get a good look, but, I mean, he *might* have been.'

The answer came not from the twins but from Urin, sitting up front near the blackboard. Her tone, however, was anything but serious.

'So then . . . What? You're saying if you get disqualified, you might actually die?' Lisa asked with a crooked smile. Placing her hands on a waist so thin you would think she had pulled a few bones from her body, she stared across at the twins' tense faces.

No one seemed to be taking the situation seriously yet. For that matter, neither was Mishin. A vague fear hung in the air, but nothing deeper than that. And while Mr Akiyama had been disqualified, none of the other game-like rules Ms Suzuta had described had actually come into play yet.

'Honestly, I don't get it either, but I'm tired. Can I just go home?' Lara Kagahi moaned like this was all someone else's problem, ruining her handsome features with a huge yawn.

'You can't leave the classroom, Lara! You'll be disqualified . . .' Sarasa Hoshikawa grabbed her arm, her voice breaking into tears.

All they really knew so far was that leaving the classroom meant disqualification.

Watching the Alpha Girls argue back and forth felt like watching a TV drama.

The next moment, there came the sudden scrape of a chair directly beside Mishin.

'For now, why don't we pair up?'

Dropping that suggestion into the chaos was Lutsu Kanamori.

'. . . What? Prez? Have you lost your mind? You're not serious, are you?' Lisa glared at her, batting her long fake eyelashes.

Lutsu let out a small breath, pushed her glasses back into place with her finger, and started speaking. 'I couldn't see what happened to Mr Akiyama from my seat in the back row, so I don't know exactly what *disqualified* means. But if – *if* – being disqualified really does mean dying, then according to the rules on the board, if we don't finish the game before the graduation ceremony starts at ten, we'll *all* die. That means we only have one hour. If we assume someone gets left out and disqualified after each round, then simple math says we can only spend just over two minutes per round . . . And it's already been three minutes since Ms Suzuta left.'

- The lesson will last for sixty minutes.
- If no graduates are decided before the ceremony, everyone will be disqualified.

Mishin checked the rules written on the board, then glanced at the clock.

Just as Lutsu had said, the hands pointed to 9:03.

'So, basically, you're telling us all to just go die?' Lisa flared.

Lutsu, however, shook her head. 'I'm only laying out the situation as it is . . .'

'What's with that tone? You trying to piss me off? Are you calling me stupid?'

Lisa thew her chair back and marched toward Lutsu's desk, ready for a fight – until Sarasa, sitting behind her, jumped to her feet and grabbed her by the arm.

'Calm down, Lisa, okay? Just think for a second. I know I freaked out when Akiyama collapsed like that, but if you think about it, there's no way being disqualified means you're going to die.

I mean, it's graduation day. Parents are coming. If twenty-five people really did die all of a sudden, that would be a massacre. Osuzu even said she'd done this before. If students had actually died that time, it would've been all over the news. But I've never heard of anything like that.'

Right.

Mishin caught her breath, suddenly remembering. Her mum was supposed to be coming to the graduation ceremony today.

'Exactly! You're totally right!' Urin, chin propped on her desk as she fiddled with her out-of-service phone, leapt to her feet. 'Yeah, there's no way we're gonna die. So, since we've got no signal and nothing better to do, why don't we just go along with the prez's idea and pair up already? And if, by some chance, whoever's left out really does drop dead – wouldn't that be *hilarious*?'

She tossed the words out to the entire classroom, then chuckled to herself like it was all a joke.

Hilarious. The word made Mishin's chest ache.

'What the hell's so funny, Urin? And don't say crap about dying. That's stupid.'

'Come on, Sarasa. Think about it. How often do you get to experience a real-life battle royale? This is insane! In a good way! If we had signal right now, I'd be live-streaming this for sure. Oh wait – I just had a genius idea. I can record it!'

Mishin knew she was only saying that because the thought of her finding herself left out hadn't so much as crossed her mind.

As Urin hummed to herself while setting up her phone camera, Sarasa crouched down miserably beside her.

'This is the worst . . . Why did something this stupid have to happen to us?'

She wasn't the only one who wanted to scream it out. But even now, only the Alpha Girls had the right to speak freely in class.

The other so-called Groundlings were probably watching with cold, detached eyes. Just like Mishin was.

'I don't want to die . . .' Sarasa's emotional cry echoed through the room.

With no warning, no cue, no preparation, the first round got underway.

'If we pair up, you won't,' Lara said calmly, and then took Sarasa's hand.

That was the trigger.

All at once, screams erupted throughout the room as their classmates leapt from their seats.

Just like Sarasa, everyone had rattled off reasons why this couldn't be a death game – but deep down, they had all been terrified. The second Ms Suzuta left, they were all desperate to grab someone's hand, just to feel safe.

Mishin's classmates rushed between desks, sprinting to their friends as the classroom broke out into an earth-shaking roar.

Mishin was still unable to move. All she could think about was Sports Day – the way she never joined in, the way she was left watching her classmates from far afield. The scene in front of her now felt exactly like that moment after the starting pistol fired.

One after another, the other students locked hands.

Alpha Girls with other Alpha Girls.

Beta Girls with others from their respective friend groups.

Even the Groundlings were sticking together.

Before she knew it, almost everyone was paired up.

The only ones left were Mishin herself, the four student council members – Karen, Lutsu, Nichika and Nodoka – and two of the Beta Girls, Aria Urushibara and Noa Ichinose.

Still rooted to the spot, Mishin finally began to feel real fear.

No matter how she thought about it, she was the one who would be left out.

The student-council members would, of course, pair off among themselves. Not even Karen would extend a hand of mercy in a situation like this. If pairing with Mishin meant Lutsu ended up left over, it wouldn't just be like pairing with Akiyama – her best friend might die.

'Let's pair up, Noa.'

Out of breath, Aria stretched out her hand across the aisle

toward Noa, sitting by the window in the last row. Mishin had never spoken to them, but after three years in the same classroom, even she knew they were close friends.

Of course. That was how it had to be. It had been obvious from the start.

Because all along, she was always the one left out.

Mishin took a small breath, then stood up.

She walked toward the window – not to watch those two clasp hands, but to look outside at the flowerbeds. The flowerbeds she had poured three years of love and care into.

It's fine. I'm not afraid.

She stared at the blossoms, still blooming strong against the heavy rain. Even if she really did die, she would just become a flower. Something beautiful, like the snowdrops that Karen loved so much. That was what she tried to tell herself.

Mishin shut her eyes, and behind her eyelids, she watched as she grew older, imagining herself running a little flower shop.

Karen would come in to buy flowers. She would arrange a bouquet. A bouquet that would suit her perfectly . . .

Warmth touched her hand. In her daydream, it was Karen accepting the bouquet with a smile. But the feeling was real – someone *was* holding her hand.

Mishin's heart thundered harder than it ever had before.

Karen.

She whispered her name in her heart as she turned.

'. . . Why?'

But it wasn't Karen holding her hand.

And the words hadn't come from Mishin, either.

'Noa? Why?'

It was Aria.

What was happening? Mishin's hand was joined with Noa's. Why would she choose to reach out to *her*, at the very bottom of the class, over her best friend, standing directly in front of her? Mishin couldn't make sense of it.

'Noa . . . We're best friends . . . Right?' Aria's voice shook.

'Yeah,' Noa answered with that soft, refined smile of hers.

'Then why are you partnering with Mizushima? If I'm the one left over, I could die . . .'

'Yeah.' Noa nodded again, still smiling, as Aria turned paler and paler.

Stuck between the two of them, Mishin's breath caught. Out of the corner of her eye, she could see the student council members quietly linking hands among themselves.

'You're saying you don't care if I die . . .?'

'Yeah.' Noa nodded once more – and this time, she broke into a full, radiant smile.

And then it started.

The yellow rose corsage pinned to Aria's chest gave off a sharp electronic beep, like a heart monitor, and its petals began to fall.

'What . . .?'

The beeping grew louder, like a countdown, each pulse sending another petal fluttering down.

- Anyone who cannot pair up will be disqualified.

When Mishin had closed her eyes by the window just minutes earlier, she hadn't really believed in death. Somewhere inside, she had thought even if she was disqualified, it couldn't possibly mean dying. Most of the class had probably thought the same. At worst, it would happen to someone else, like watching a movie, a tragedy befalling other people.

But now, she felt it with absolute clarity. This was disqualification. This was a death countdown.

'What do I do, Noa . . .? I'm not actually going to die, am I? There's no way I'm going to die over something like this, right . . .?' Aria stumbled forward, her thought spilling out in panic. 'Noa, please – just let go of Mizushima already. Take *my* hand!' She lunged forward, arm outstretched, desperation etched into her movements.

But Noa didn't let go of Mishin's hand.

And she didn't take Aria's, either.

Before she could answer – Aria's left side was blown away.

The scattered petals from her corsage fell onto Mishin, while the remnants of Aria's shattered left torso rained down on Noa's head. Her right side and head were still intact.

'Hyeeeaaahhh!'

The raw, grotesque scene drew screams that piled on top of one another, a chorus of terror.

The close-range explosion had rattled Mishin's eardrums. Nonetheless, she was probably the only one who heard what Noa murmured amid the shrieking.

'. . . Best friends, huh?'

Mishin knew what yellow roses meant in the language of flowers.

Friendship. And jealousy.

- The moment you take someone's hand, you will be officially paired with them.

Round 1

Sarasa Hoshikawa - Lara Kagahi
Lisa Okami - Urin Nekoya
Yayoi Yoitani - Kiko Masugi
Sayuki Sena -
Uta Marguerite Samejima
Yuki Koiwai - Katsune Nakano
Yu Nikaido - Leika Tomoe
Sui Inoue - Aoi Morita
Moe Fuyuno - Inori Rokujo
Setsuna Kuroki - Natsuki Himuro
Umi Hagiwara - Hime Shirayuki
Lutsu Kanamori - Nodoka Saeki
Karen Asakura - Nichika Saeki
Noa Ichinose - Mishin Mizushima

Disqualified:
Aria Urushibara

Students Remaining: 26

Time Left:
52 minutes

Chapter 2: Best Friends

Noa Ichinose

'. . . Why?'

Aria Urushibara's dying voice echoed in Noa's ears.

Noa brushed a scrap of Aria's flesh from her hair, as if shaking off a newborn ghost.

'. . . Why?'

This time, the voice that trembled faintly amid her classmates' screams didn't belong to Aria.

The fading whisper came from Mishin Mizushima.

Overwhelmed with adrenaline, Noa finally let go of the hand she had still been holding onto – Mishin's.

That *why* was probably asking why Noa had taken *her* hand. Or maybe it was asking why she had betrayed Aria, her best friend.

After steadying her breath, Noa faced Mishin and answered clearly, 'Because I wanted her gone.'

Mishin stared at her, speechless. It was little wonder. Anyone would have said that Noa and Aria were best friends. Yes – best friends, without a doubt. Yet even now, as she faced her best friend's death, she didn't feel so much as a hint of sadness. But for Noa, that seemed perfectly natural.

'I always hated her.'

Ever since the day they met.

Almost ten years had passed since then – ten years she had spent standing beside Aria, wearing a fake smile and hiding her true feelings.

She had regretted it ever since – that spring day, just after they had started third grade at elementary school, during that lunch break.

If she hadn't spoken to her then, they never would have become *best friends*.

Even back then, there were a few little groups in their classroom.

It wasn't anything like a rigid social hierarchy, with clear first-, second- and third-tier groups – just something more instinctive. Noa had simply fallen in with kids she kind of got along with – those who seemed to come from similar homes or lived nearby. That was why she could barely remember their faces, was no longer connected to any of them on social media and didn't care what they were doing. It was that superficial – too tenuous to call friendship.

The reason Aria had been left out of every group back then wasn't bullying or anything like that – it was because she had just transferred in from another school.

Seeing her spend a whole week alone during lunch had made Noa feel sorry for her.

'Hey, Aria, wanna come play with us?'

When Noa invited her to join them that day, it wasn't because she wanted to be close – it was just the kind of simple kindness any child might offer.

'. . . Really? You're sure?'

Even now, Noa could picture Aria's face at that moment – bright and blooming like a flower. She hardly remembered anything else from elementary school in such detail, but she remembered that conversation word for word.

'Yeah, of course.'

'Thank you. I'm happy you remembered my name . . .'

'Well, it's hard to forget. *Aria* sounds kinda foreign, like you're from overseas. I think that every time the teacher calls attendance.'

'. . . You think it's weird?'

'Weird? It's not weird. It's beautiful. That's why I remembered it.'

'. . . You're really nice, Noa.'

'Huh? No, not really. I'm just normal.'

Back then, she hadn't even been alive ten years, and she had never thought of herself as a kind person. She just couldn't leave a lonely girl isolated and alone.

From that day on, Aria naturally became part of Noa's group. Children adapted with frightening ease. Before long, it was as if she had always been there. She had transferred from rural Nara, so compared to the other kids, she was plain, a little chubby and simple-looking – but none of that made her unlikeable. Noa didn't know what it meant to really *dislike* someone back then.

But over and over, she thought – she never should have taken that hand. She should have pushed her out of her life much, much sooner.

'Morning, Noa. It's freezing today, huh?'

That morning, when Noa stepped outside to head to school, Aria was standing in front of the plum tree her mother tended in the yard – or rather, she was *waiting* for her.

'Oh . . . Yeah. Morning.'

Noa was taken aback. She already knew Aria lived nearby since their group had walked home together several times before. If they had just bumped into each other, that would have been fine. She certainly hadn't expected Aria to wait for her on purpose. Yet Aria acted like it was perfectly normal – as if they had always walked to school together.

Smiling, Aria held out her hand. 'C'mon, Noa, let's go!'

'Uh . . . Yeah.'

Noa hesitated before taking it. They hadn't made any promise to walk together, but she couldn't bring herself to ignore someone who had come out of her way to meet up with her.

'Oh, your friend came to pick you up? Isn't that nice, Noa?'

But when her mother said that as she saw them off, Noa was struck by a feeling of discomfort. It didn't *feel* nice at all. She had barely ever talked to Aria one-on-one, and in their group, she was closer with the other girls.

'I'm Aria Urushibara,' Aria said, bowing politely to her mother.

'What a lovely name,' her mother replied.

And yes – Noa had once thought so herself.

But from that day on, that name began to sound almost frightening. Starting the very next day, Aria came to pick her up again – and every single morning after that, rain or shine, without ever being asked.

'I had the weirdest dream last night, Noa.'

'Oh yeah? What kind?'

'I dreamed Matsuzaka from the other class said he liked me! You know, he's *super* good-looking, and he's the most popular boy among all the girls. I was so shocked I woke up!'

Aria never said much when they were with the group, but once they were alone, she turned into a chatterbox – almost always about romance. Actually, *only* about romance. She was forever crushing on the kind of popular boys who wouldn't even notice girls like them.

All the way to school, Noa listened to Aria's cotton-candy stories of impossible crushes – fluffy, empty and dissolving the moment they touched air. Aria never asked Noa a single question, never showed any interest in her. She just talked and talked. It was nothing if not exhausting. And again – Noa had never agreed to walk to school with her.

But saying no to an innocent invitation like that felt impossibly hard.

'I'm really glad we're best friends, Noa.'

Before she knew it, Aria had started calling them *best friends*.

We're not best friends, Noa wanted to scream. But she couldn't say it out loud. She didn't have it in her to be that cruel.

Soon, her so-called *best friend* started coming over to play at her house.

Noa's mother took special care of Aria – probably out of pity. Her mother, too, was the kind of person who couldn't ignore someone in need.

Noa herself had realized that Aria's home life was complicated.

It wasn't that her family was poor or abusive. The problem was that her parents had completely fallen out of love, yet stayed married anyway. When Noa visited Aria's apartment, her parents didn't even bother to hide their affairs – if *affair* was the right word for it. And neither of them was the type to show affection toward their child. Aria had never once gone anywhere as a family.

When Noa's mother heard about her circumstances, she held Aria's hand with teary eyes and said, 'That must be so hard on you.' Then, she invited her to the Ichinose family's annual summer camping trip.

Of course, Aria was thrilled. It was her first campfire, and she was more excited than anyone. And the next year, and the year after that, she joined as if it were her right. Noa had wanted to spend that time with her family – but her mother kept saying, 'Make sure you invite Aria,' so she had no choice.

After giving birth to Noa by emergency caesarean, her mother had been told she couldn't have any more children. She often said she wished she could have raised sisters, so maybe she was using Aria to fill that void – and because of that, Noa couldn't entirely blame Aria.

'We're just like real sisters, huh?' Aria said joyfully while they lay under the ceiling of the two-person tent her father had bought so they could have their own space.

You're always getting in my way, Noa thought in her heart that night. She wanted to sleep in the same tent as her parents. She couldn't understand why she had to share a tent with someone she didn't even consider a friend, let alone a *best* friend.

'Yeah,' she answered anyway.

She kept agreeing, because she was afraid – afraid that if she hurt Aria, she would end up hurting herself.

She knew it was her own fault. Her inability to shake off Aria had let this *best friendship* drag on all the way into high school.

'Hey, Noa, let's be partners.'

Pair up however you like, the gym teacher called out – and Aria always came running straight to her, desperate.

She seemed terrified of being left alone.

Maybe that was because she had grown up unloved – or maybe, deep down, she had already sensed how Noa truly felt.

'Yeah.'

And Noa kept taking that hand – because it was the only one left. She didn't want to end up like Mishin, isolated and unwanted.

'Hey, Noa, let's always stay best friends, okay?'

For nearly ten years, Noa kept nodding along to those words. Lately, she had stopped even thinking about it.

Everyone already saw them as best friends. Besides, this wouldn't last forever. Once they graduated high school, it would finally be over. A little more patience, that was all she needed.

Noa had decided to go to nursing school. Aria, being easily swayed, seemed dead set on attending college. She was always going on about how she wanted to experience campus life like in the old drama *Orange Days*, and about how much she wanted a boyfriend.

But then, one day –

'Hey Noa, I decided I'm going to go to the same nursing school as you! I saw a rerun of that show *Nurses in Action* the other day, and being a nurse looked so fun – and they're popular, too, right? And doctors are *so* hot!'

And that was that.

Noa couldn't stand how shallow it was – to treat a profession that dealt with people's lives like some kind of trend. *In the way* wasn't even enough anymore. She wanted Aria gone. Gone from her sight, gone from her life.

'Let's always be best friends, okay?'

That phrase had become a curse.

But now she was dead. Noa was finally free of that cursed friendship.

Beside Aria's body – missing her left shoulder and everything below it – Noa finally felt like herself again.

'*Best friends*, huh? What a joke,' she said, smiling at Mishin.

In the now-silent classroom, the only sound was quiet sobbing born of fear. It was only natural – one of their classmates was dead, and the word *disqualified* had just been proven to be code for *death*. In all likelihood, Noa was the only one who felt calm.

As the others, minds shut down in terror, began pairing up with whoever was still free in their groups –

'W-wait, please.'

The one who stopped them was Lutsu Kanamori. Judging by her overly serious appearance, she should have ranked in the lower half of the Beta Girls socially, but she was the smartest in the class, and had served as student council president, so people respected her. Like Noa, she sat somewhere in the middle of the second tier.

'This time . . . there's an even number of us. According to the rules on the board, we can't start the second round until we decide who's going to sit out,' Lutsu explained. Even with her face stiffened by fear, her voice remained calm and composed.

Noa looked up at the blackboard.

- If the remaining number is even, one person must sit out. (The person to sit out will be decided by vote.)

Yes, that was indeed one of the rules.

'. . . Seriously, can we just stop this already? We all know now that *disqualified* means dead – how can we keep playing this sick game?!' Sarasa Hoshikawa, queen of the Alpha Girls, shouted dramatically like some movie heroine.

'She's right. Let's stop. I don't wanna die.'

'Yeah, let's just quit.'

Voices of agreement rose from all over the room. Noa didn't say anything, but she was silently agreeing with them.

That, however, was short-lived.

'. . . But if we don't finish within the time limit, it's possible we'll *all* die . . .'

With that grim comment from Lutsu, the classroom fell quiet again.

For the longest moment, the silence was filled only by the sound of the pouring rain outside.

'Okay, *sooo*, let's put the whole *keep going or not* thing aside for now and just do a vote to decide who's gonna be the standby person, yeah?' Urin Nekoya's bright voice cut through the funereal atmosphere.

Her eyes flicked toward the smartphone camera set up under the calligraphy scroll emblazoned with the word *Hope* at the back of the room. It wasn't hard to imagine that, in her YouTuber brain, this ordeal was already being converted into view counts.

'Alrighty then, please vote for the person you think deserves to survive!'

The one who deserves to survive.

As Urin's words sank in, Noa found herself glancing toward Karen Asakura.

Karen sat staring out at the rain with eyes like those of an abandoned kitten.

When she had first transferred in, her beauty had been so overwhelming that Noa couldn't help but imagine – if Aria had been that kind of delicate, lovely new girl, she probably would have been happy to be her friend.

And not just because Karen was beautiful on the outside – her heart was beautiful, as well.

Incredibly, she had sometimes even chosen to pair up with Mishin, the class's forgotten ghost. Not every time, but whenever Karen took Mishin's hand, she made that ignored, unseen girl visible again.

Noa felt a pang in her chest. On the one hand, she didn't want to end up like Mishin, but on the other, part of her wanted to reach out to her, like Karen did. Noa had always been that kind of person – kind by nature. In the end, however, she had never acted on it. Partly because she always had to pair with Aria, but mostly because she was afraid that showing kindness would make someone cling to her again.

'Hold on!' Lutsu, panicked, shouted over Urin's reckless call. 'Everyone, look at the rules on the blackboard again! The section that says *If the designated student is purposefully excluded by the others*!'

- If the **designated student** is purposefully excluded by the others, then everyone except that student will be disqualified.

Noa gasped. Even if she was acting calm, the truth was, she was caught up in the chaos like everyone else. No one could think clearly enough to check the rules carefully or consider what that line actually meant.

'Huh . . . So, who exactly is this *designated student* supposed to be?' Lisa Okami muttered irritably, eyes on the blackboard.

'If you think about it rationally . . . it must mean the student who's *always* been left out,' Lutsu answered nervously.

Noa turned to look at Mishin beside her. Everyone did.

Lutsu was right. If this special class really was part of an anti-bullying campaign, then the phrase *designated student* could only refer to Mishin.

Which meant . . . if Noa hadn't taken Mishin's hand earlier, everyone except her would have been disqualified, including herself.

'Let me get this straight – you *wanted* this stupid game, didn't you?' Lisa demanded like nobility addressing a commoner.

Mishin shook her head, clearly terrified.

This was the first time in all three years of high school that she had seen any of the Alpha Girls speaking to her.

'But you're the one who wrote that you didn't want to be paired with Akiyama on the survey, right? I mean, it's gotta be you.'

After about five seconds of silence, Mishin gave a small, defeated nod. Her frail body trembled, no doubt from fear. Noa knew she would have reacted the same way if Lisa were in her face like that.

'Then that makes *you* the perp. *You're* the one who wrote there's bullying in this class, aren't you? This whole mess is because of *you*.'

It wasn't an unreasonable accusation, but it was a cruel one.

Once again, Lutsu tried to restore order. 'Calm down, Okami. Even if that *were* true, blaming Mizushima won't change anything. We're running out of time . . . Like Nekoya suggested, let's put aside whether we keep playing and just vote – keeping that *designated student* rule in mind.'

Lisa clicked her tongue, making the already awful atmosphere worse. 'Suit yourselves.'

Noa could feel Lisa's frustration seeping out of her. Deep down, she wished Lisa would be the next to die.

'Hey, Lisa-Lisa. Your followers are gonna drop if you keep being that cranky.' Urin, now holding the phone that had been fixed at the back of the room, turned the camera on Lisa with a teasing grin.

'What followers? And stop calling me that – it's cringe.'

'Ha-ha-ha, sorry, sorry. But you know, I'm recording this right now! You should probably talk like the whole world's watching!'

'Are you an idiot? You can't stream this. Someone literally died. There's a corpse right there. You'd get banned instantly.'

'I'll just edit or blur that part out later.'

'Do you even care if it blows up in your face?'

'I keep telling you, my popularity can survive a little controversy.' Laughing, Urin hopped up onto the teacher's desk and aimed her camera at the whole room. 'Okaaay! Let's start the vote! If you want Mishin Mizushima to sit this one out, raise your hand!'

Given how bubbly and light-hearted she was, she sounded like she was announcing the theme for the school culture festival.

Almost everyone's hand went up. So did Noa's. There was no need to count.

'Alrighty then, the standby for this round is Mizushima!' Urin declared brightly.

That was when the gunshot rang out for the second time.

It hadn't really mattered whether they debated or not – the outcome had been decided from the start. If they didn't finish in time, no one would survive.

Once again, the students started pairing off, swapping partners within their groups.

All Noa could do was stand beside Mishin and watch.

Was this punishment for betraying her best friend, or for pretending to be one?

For ten years, Noa had lived under Aria's shadow. She didn't belong to any group anymore. She was, inevitably, the one left over.

Less than thirty seconds after the second round began, the flower on Noa's chest started to fall apart, its petals dropping one by one with a sound like a flatlining heart monitor. Exactly as had happened just before.

As she watched the petals drift away, Noa smiled. It wasn't that she was happy – she just didn't know what other expression to wear.

'Hey, Noa, let's be partners.'

The voice came right next to her ear, just as the last petal fell.

Aria stood there, her left side blown away, smiling, and reaching out with her uninjured right hand. Was this a hallucination, or the work of a newborn ghost? Noa couldn't tell anymore. All she knew was that if she took that hand, she would be dragged straight down to hell.

'Hey Noa, let's always stay best friends, okay?'

She had hated her.

So why were tears falling at those cursed words? She didn't need to think about it. She already knew.

In the end, Aria was all she had ever had.

For better or worse, no one else had ever wanted her so completely.

'Yeah.'

And so, Noa took her hand again.

Round 2

Standby: Mishin Mizushima

Sarasa Hoshikawa - Urin Nekoya
Lisa Okami - Lara Kagahi
Kiko Masugi -
Uta Marguerite Samejima
Sayuki Sena - Yayoi Yoitani
Karen Asakura - Nodoka Saeki
Lutsu Kanamori - Nichika Saeki
Yuki Koiwai - Yu Nikaido
Leika Tomoe - Katsune Nakano
Aoi Morita - Inori Rokujo
Moe Fuyuno - Sui Inoue
Setsuna Kuroki - Hime Shirayuki
Natsuki Himuro - Umi Hagiwara

Disqualified:
Noa Ichinose

Students Remaining: 25

Time Left:
46 minutes

Chapter 3: Trio

Aoi Morita

It might be me who dies next time . . .

Aoi Morita quivered in terror before the corpse of Noa Ichinose, who had collapsed over Aria Urushibara's blood-soaked body after being disqualified in the previous round.

'Let's pair up next, Inori.'

'Yeah. Definitely.'

Right in front of her, Sui Inoue and Inori Rokujo – her fellow light music club members – made that promise to each other.

Aoi's breath hitched. Since entering the school, she had always been with these two. The three of them were, in every sense, a trio.

It wasn't that Inori and Midori were excluding her. Aoi had paired with Midori in the first round, and with Inori in the second. It was only natural that when the third round began, Inori and Midori, who hadn't yet paired with each other, would join hands.

'. . . Since the number of students is odd this time, we won't need to vote for someone to sit out,' Lutsu Kanamori announced coldly from the teacher's desk.

And the second round had only just ended.

Aoi knew Lutsu hadn't wanted this, hadn't set up the game. She was just taking responsibility – acting out of the same sense of duty that had made her student council president. Still, as someone who might die when the game resumed, Lutsu's figure struck her as an emissary from hell.

'Now . . . there are forty-six minutes left.'

That was clearly the signal that the third round was about to begin.

Footsteps echoed across the damaged classroom floor. None of the students understood what this special lesson was really supposed to mean. They couldn't. The only thing driving them was the will to live.

Aoi looked around.

Once again, the Alpha Girls and the other Beta Girls were pairing off without trouble.

Right. If you were in a group of four, the third round was simple – you simply paired with whoever you hadn't paired with already.

But in our case . . .

Crushed by despair, Aoi sank to the floor.

'Inori.'

'Sui.'

The two called out each other's names and joined hands.

Three-person groups are the worst, Aoi thought again, watching on.

Aoi and the others had entered high school on 7 April 2016.

Back then, there were usually two types of girls who joined the light music club without any prior musical experience – those inspired by the wildly popular manga and anime series *K-On!*, or those who genuinely wanted to learn how to play music.

Aoi belonged to the former group. She chose drums because she loved Ritsu Tainaka, the drummer from the anime.

She had watched the show as an elementary schooler, and she had wanted to join a band in middle school, too. But her co-ed school's club was full of experienced boys, and the atmosphere made it impossible for a clueless girl to join.

This high school, on the other hand, had only about eighty students in total, and since it was all girls, the light music club was practically dead – which made it the perfect place for her long-awaited debut.

Aoi had dreamed of a life straight out of that anime – lazy tea times after school, writing lyrics together, composing original songs and performing them at the culture festival to thunderous applause.

But within a month of joining, she had learned two harsh truths.

First, anime was just anime. And second, the girls in that show weren't awkward, low-tier nerds like her – they were beautiful, unique and effortlessly cool. Real Alpha Girls.

'Hey, Midori, did you see PinocchioP's new song on Niconico yesterday?'

'Yeah. It's amazing.'

'I know, right? I've been playing it on repeat all day.'

Midori and Inori worshiped Vocaloid music. Like Aoi, they hadn't joined because of a love for instruments, but because they were nerds at heart. They idolized the Vocaloid scene – the producers, the cover singers, the *tried playing* musicians. Inori, who had the best voice, became the guitarist and singer. Midori picked bass.

'Oh, I heard it, too. It's so good!' Aoi exclaimed, jumping into the conversation.

The truth was, she hadn't listened to the song at all. She preferred YouTube over Niconico, and she was never really into Vocaloid in the first place. But she hated feeling left out, so pretending to know what they were talking about had become second nature.

She *did* try to fit in – listening to popular tracks, adding *K-On!* songs like 'Fluffy Time' to their setlist for the cultural festival, even though she mostly went along with whatever songs the other two liked. One of them, 'Hated by Life Itself', was their absolute favourite. It was hard to play – *really* hard – but since Aoi had already blurted, 'That's *my* favourite, too,' there was no backing out.

'Wait, Aoi, you checked out PinocchioP's new one as well? It's so good, huh?'

'Yeah, totally! We should cover it!'

Whenever she faked knowing a song, she prayed they wouldn't ask which part she liked best. Strangely, they never did. Maybe they had seen through her all along.

Now, as Aoi sat dazed on the floor, pairs formed all around her. The sight was less cruel than surreal. Even with two bodies already lying on the ground, it still didn't sink in that they were caught up in a death game.

Only a nameless, bottomless fear filled her chest. Her thoughts started to fade, her consciousness drifting away – until suddenly, something snapped her back.

A figure came into view, and she remembered – she still had a chance to survive.

Fighting dizziness, she staggered toward the windows.

'. . . Hey, Fuyuno, will you pair up with me?'

She approached Moe Fuyuno, standing alone in a corner.

Moe had paired with Inori in the first round, and with Midori in the second. That meant she would surely pair with Aoi this time. Aoi had completely forgotten about her in the chaos, but she didn't need to worry anymore.

Yet Moe's answer was immediate. 'No.'

'Huh . . .? But you already paired with Midori and Inori, right?'

'Yeah.'

'Then why not . . .?'

Aoi was taken aback. She hadn't imagined being refused. Moe was near the very bottom of the class hierarchy – right above Mishin Mizushima. She didn't have many friends. As proof of that, she wasn't holding hands with anyone this round.

And yet, there wasn't a trace of urgency in her voice.

'Morita. You're probably thinking, *I'm being nice enough to offer to partner up with you*, right?' Moe accused her, her tone almost smug.

Aoi instinctively stepped back. 'That's not what I meant . . .'

'Heh. Thought so,' Moe shot back, her gaze sharp enough to cut. 'You're always like that – only ever thinking about yourself.' Covering her mouth with a wrinkled sleeve, she let out a quiet, mocking laugh.

What on earth was this? Why was she being attacked out of nowhere by someone she barely even talked to? Aoi could feel her temper flaring.

Her voice turned cold. 'Look, we barely even talk. How could you possibly know what I'm like?'

She *hated* it when people pretended to know her.

'Well, you've never once paired with me in gym class, have you?'

It was true. Aoi had never been partners with Moe. But that was just because they weren't close. There was no deeper reason behind it.

'So what?'

'You really don't get it?' Moe sighed, tilting her head. 'When the teacher says, *Pair up,* your little trio always leaves one person out. And the leftover one always ends up coming to me, looking all apologetic. But not you. Not once. You always make sure it's either Rokujo or Inoue who's left out, so *you* never have to be. You know those two are best friends, right? And yet, for three full years, you never once let them pair together. Don't you feel even a little guilty?'

At this, a tear rolled down Aoi's cheek. Her chest hurt, like it had been torn open.

She had been pretending not to notice.

That Inori and Sui seemed happier when they talked to each other.

That she was the unnecessary one in the group.

She just hadn't wanted to admit it.

Aoi had always thought she was the prettiest and most stylish of the three. Sure, she had gotten into the club because of *K-On!*, but she wasn't really a nerd on their level. This was an all-girls school, so she hadn't dated anyone here, but back in middle school she had even had a boyfriend for a month – he wasn't handsome, but still. She liked clothes, romance movies, even TVXQ. She was, in her mind, a perfectly normal high school girl.

If it weren't for her, Inori and Sui – those two *obvious* nerds – would have made the light music club a laughing stock. Performing Vocaloid songs at the festival would have been beyond embarrassing. She was the one who showed them hair salons, took them shopping, gave them fashion and makeup tips. Without her, they would still be awkward geeks – Groundling nobodies.

They should have been grateful she had befriended them. And

when one of them inevitably got left out during gym class, she had felt it was just the natural order of things.

To be blunt – she had looked down on them. Even though she herself wasn't an Alpha Girl.

Still, Aoi had always believed she had what it took to be special. If the light music club had just been a little more glamorous, she *could* have been an Alpha Girl – maybe even someone like Ritsu Tainaka.

But a year ago, that illusion was shattered when Karen Asakura transferred in.

Karen had something none of the other Alpha Girls did – a *presence*, like she had stepped out of a story. Just by existing, she made everything around her feel cinematic. And that was something Aoi knew *she* would never have. Only people like that could be the main characters.

'I'll pair with Mizushima. Good luck.'

Moe's voice was cold, emotionless.

Even now, it hadn't occurred to Aoi to pair with Mishin Mizushima, the lowest of the low. She hadn't even considered it. To her, Mizushima wasn't a *designated student* or anything special – just a ghost.

Then came the merciless mechanical tone – the sound of death. Yellow petals scattered from her chest, fluttering down like ash.

'Heh.'

A dry laugh escaped her rotten heart.

In the end, it had all been ego. Even transforming Inori and Sui's looks hadn't been for them – it had been to create her ideal version of the light music club.

And now, because of that ego, she was being disqualified. If Inori and Sui had just paired first, she wouldn't have been left out like this.

Wordlessly, Aoi walked toward the two of them – who, for the first time in three years, were finally holding hands.

'I'm sorry, Aoi.'

'Sorry . . . Aoi . . .'

They spoke weakly, looking down at her, their hands tightly clasped. They were taller – about one hundred and sixty centimetres to her one hundred and fifty – and slimmer, too.

'You'll both be dead soon anyway!' Aoi shouted, pointing at them.

Even after three years together, she could tell – they weren't truly sad she was dying. That was what hurt more than anything.

But . . . if *they* had been the ones dying first, would *she* have felt genuine grief?

'. . . I'm the worst,' she muttered.

Because she wouldn't have.

Because she hadn't loved them.

Not them. Not the music they loved.

Aoi had only ever wanted the kind of youth girls in anime had – the perfect, glossy version.

Round 3

Sarasa Hoshikawa - Lisa Okami
Urin Nekoya - Lara Kagahi
Yayoi Yoitani - Karen Asakura
Kiko Masugi - Lutsu Kanamori
Sayuki Sena - Nichika Saeki
Nodoka Saeki -
Uta Marguerite Samejima
Yuki Koiwai - Leika Tomoe
Katsune Nakano - Yu Nikaido
Setsuna Kuroki - Umi Hagiwara
Natsuki Himuro - Hime Shirayuki
Inori Rokujo - Sui Inoue
Moe Fuyuno - Mishin Mizushima

Disqualified:
Aoi Morita

Students Remaining: 24

Time Left:
42 minutes

Chapter 4: Groundlings
Hime Shirayuki

Hime steadied her breathing.

The third round had ended before she could even make sense of what was happening. Even though no one had been running around the classroom since the second round, simply standing still had left her out of breath.

It felt like ages since this special lesson, this graduation game, had begun – but when she checked the clock, only eighteen minutes had passed. In that short time, three of her classmates had already been *disqualified*.

Each of their deaths had been gruesome enough to make anyone look away, but there didn't seem to be any pattern to them.

The corsage lodged deep in Aoi Morita's chest was soaked in blood.

Noa Ichinose, who had died in the second round, had likely been injected with poison – she had vomited blood until she at last went still.

And Aria Urushibara, the first to die, had exploded, her upper left body shattered from the neck down. Hime couldn't imagine how any of it worked, but it was clear that every corsage had a different mechanism inside.

If she was to avoid being disqualified herself, she would have to remove that cheap-looking fake rose pinned with a little *Congratulations on Graduating!* tag.

Hime gently cupped the flower blooming on her left chest in her palm.

- Anyone who removes their corsage will be disqualified.

Remembering that rule, she stopped herself.

Before the game had truly started, Mr Akiyama had ignored another of the rules and stepped out of the classroom, resulting in his immediate disqualification. If she remembered correctly, it was right after Ms Suzuta had placed a corsage onto his chest.

Hime pulled her hand away from the petals and shook her head.

Removing the corsage meant instant death. Based on what she had seen so far, there was no doubt about that.

And yet, even after watching three of her classmates die, death still didn't feel *real* to her.

Maybe it was because, by some miracle, every single one of the Groundling girls – herself included – was still alive.

Hime glanced at Natsuki Himuro, her partner from the last round.

In all three rounds, Hime had only paired with other third-tier girls. That meant Natsuki was one of them, too. To put it simply, Natsuki was gloomy – so gloomy it was as if those black vertical lines from the manga series *Chibi Maruko-chan* were hanging behind her at all times.

When she first introduced herself, she had mentioned that both her parents had died in an accident years ago and she now lived in a children's home. Hime didn't know the details, but she figured that was probably the reason for her darkness.

In addition to Natsuki, there was another girl in their class who lived in the same children's home – Setsuna Kuroki, the girl Hime had paired with two rounds ago.

Anyone could see that Setsuna didn't look like a Groundling. She was genuinely cute. Rather, it was her strange behaviour that had led to her low social ranking.

'Don't be scared, Natsuki. People like us – we're the chosen ones.'

She had a full-blown case of what people called *edgy teen syndrome*. Her pale wrists, always wrapped in bandages, had probably never seen sunlight, and she sometimes even wore an eyepatch.

Of course, everyone talked about her behind her back. Even

Hime had joined in once or twice. But no one ever mocked her openly. Partly because she was too pitiful to target, and partly because, right after they all started in first year, she had shown up with a bruise on her face so large it looked like someone had hit her. Rumour had it she was being abused – that her weird persona was just a way of coping – and that was why she had ended up in foster care.

But it was just a rumour. Hime didn't really know the truth.

Setsuna and Natsuki always stuck together, lost in their own little world. No one could wedge themselves in between them.

In other words, just because the third-tier Groundling girls were all treated the same didn't mean they were united or close. There were levels even among them – maybe not as steep as among the Beta Girls, but levels nonetheless. And Hime knew she sat near the top. Still, unlike the higher groups, the third-tier girls quietly shared a sense that, at the very least, they were all in this together.

'You okay, Hime?'

A flat voice made her turn around. It was Umi Hagiwara, looking up at her. Because of their twenty-centimetre height difference – Hime at one hundred and sixty-five centimetres, Umi at one hundred and forty-five – Umi always had to look up when talking to her. They were both in the drama club, so it had been natural for them to pair up in the first round. Umi was also one of the higher-ranked girls within the Groundling group.

'Yeah. You?' Hime asked.

'More or less,' Umi replied.

She was normally impossible to read, her features a perfect poker face, but Hime wanted to believe this time it was forced calm. Even now, she could never quite tell what Umi was thinking.

They had spent three years in the drama club together, Hime acting in the plays Umi wrote. People said you could understand someone through their writing, but no matter how many times she read Umi's scripts, Hime couldn't figure her out. Their minds worked on completely different wavelengths.

Umi's plays were what you would call *literary* or *absurdist* – philosophical pieces that didn't care about plot. For Hime – who couldn't even fully grasp *Attack on Titan*, a manga often described as both entertainment and philosophy – Umi's writing was simply too difficult.

'But next time,' Umi said plainly, 'one of us is probably gonna die.'

Hime didn't need to ask what *us* meant. She was talking about the Groundling girls.

So far, Hime had paired with Umi, Setsuna and Natsuki. The same was true for the other three. Which meant none of them could hold hands again.

That left only one person among the third-tier girls who hadn't yet paired up – excluding Mishin Mizushima, who would probably be left sitting out again. That person was Moe Fuyuno, who always acted alone.

So, the question was – who would Moe pair with next?

Would one of the Beta Girls who had already paired with her – Inori Rokujo or Sui Inoue – offer to join with someone from their group this time?

Whoever they chose would live. The rest wouldn't. What stung most was that even now, in this nightmare, the third-tier girls still had no right to ask the higher ones to pair with them. Or maybe they just didn't have the courage.

Hime took a deep breath, trying to steady her rising panic.

She hadn't accepted this absurd situation – no one could – but she couldn't help thinking it was strange that she was still alive. Honestly, she had thought she would be the first to die. Because she didn't have any close friends. At least, not in this classroom.

Hime remembered her best friend, Emi Akanishi, who she thought about all the time.

'I'm transferring schools,' Emi told her a month before the culture festival in their second year.

They were eating lunch on the rooftop, as they always did, beneath a flawlessly clear stretch of blue unmarred by even a single cloud.

'Why?' Hime asked.

'I'm going to be an actress. I'm joining a theatre company in Tokyo.'

'You can't.'

The words shot out before she could stop them.

Emi had been in the drama club, too – and she had been good. Really good. She had even balanced it with student council work. But still, she wasn't *that* good. Not good enough to go to Tokyo.

'Why would you say that?'

'Because actresses are . . . pretty. Only pretty girls get to be actresses.'

Emi wasn't pretty. Neither was Hime, but Emi was worse.

'That's not true. Sometimes, being pretty works against you. And sometimes, being ugly's an advantage,' Emi said – not angry, just calm.

Thinking back, Hime realized she had never seen her angry. But their friendship wasn't fragile enough to break over looks. They had even jokingly called themselves the *Ugly Alliance*. They both knew exactly where they stood.

'Yeah, but still, pretty girls have way more opportunities. Even for them, it's nearly impossible to make it, so how could you?'

She must have panicked when she heard the word *transfer*, because before she knew it, she had blurted out something awful.

When she was in elementary school, Hime had been cast as Snow White in the class play.

She hadn't wanted the part. She hadn't even raised her hand for it. But because her name was Shirayuki – literally *Snow White* – the class had voted her in as a joke. Her classmates had clapped and snickered while she stood there humiliated. Because an ugly girl was playing the princess.

Looking back, there had never been a time in her life when being ugly had worked in her favour. It had only ever hurt.

'I'll make it. Definitely.'

But Emi didn't back down. She stood tall, reached her hand toward the blue sky, sunlight spilling over her, and smiled down at Hime.

'Do you remember why you joined the drama club, Hime? Wasn't it 'cause you wanted to be someone else for a while? I think the world isn't just for people born lucky. The ones who *really* make it – those are the people who know pain. Besides, I might be ugly, but I love who I am.'

Her radiant smile was full of something stronger than anger – pure conviction.

That turned out to be their last real conversation.

Until she transferred, Emi hadn't ignored her or refused to eat lunch together. But Hime could tell – her responses had become shallow, polite, surface-level.

It had been worse than a fight.

Emi left school after the culture festival, just a few days before Karen Asakura transferred in.

The classroom didn't change at all after she left, which somehow made it feel even sadder.

But the day Karen arrived, everything changed.

'Hey, Asakura, you're from Tokyo, right? Ever been to Shibuya?'

'Yeah, a few times.'

'Whoa, that's so cool!'

'Not really. Shibuya's really crowded, and it kind of stinks there.'

'But celebrities go there all the time, right?'

'Not really. You just see them filming sometimes, that's all.'

'Filming? That's awesome!'

'You know what's even cooler? I heard you can see fireflies over the Kamo River in summer. In Tokyo, you have to pay to see them.'

Because she was *beautiful*. Truly beautiful.

In that moment, Hime realized that people like her, people born with that kind of inner beauty – *those* were the ones who became actresses.

It was about a week after Karen's enrolment, right after music class.

'You've got such pretty hair, Shirayuki,' Karen had said, catching her in the bathroom mirror.

No one higher than her on the social ladder had ever complimented her looks before.

There probably wasn't a single third-tier girl who disliked Karen.

Because Karen had been kind – even to Mishin Mizushima, the class ghost. She had offered her hand without hesitation. When someone that beautiful treated you kindly, you couldn't help but feel happy. And when someone that beautiful turned cold on you, it didn't matter whether you liked her or not – it felt like being thrown into absolute darkness.

'Since we've got an even number this time, we'll first have to decide who's going to wait this round out.'

Lutsu Kanamori's voice yanked Hime Shirayuki back into a reality that could only be described as hell.

'All in favour of voting for Mishin Mizushima?'

Almost everyone raised their hands, as did Hime. There wasn't time to think, and if she had to vote for someone other than herself, it honestly didn't matter who it was.

'Hey, Katsune, let's team up with Lisa and the others.'

'Yeah, of course.'

'Then I'm pairing with Yuki!'

'Yu, partner with me!'

The Alpha Girls started teaming up with one of the Beta Girl groups – Beta Girls B, as the others called them. Both sides had four members each, so it was obvious that sticking together would keep them safer for longer.

Hime's eyes flicked toward Lara Kagahi. The girl who was practically the prince of the all-girls school wore the same cool, unshakable look she always did as she paired off with Leika Tomoe, the richest and most refined girl in class.

'Hey, Karen, will you and your group team up with us?'

Soon after, the calligraphy club group – Beta Girls A – invited the student council members, Karen Asakura, Lutsu Kanamori and Nichika and Nodoka Saeki. In the social ranking, Beta Girls A sat even higher than Beta Girls B. They weren't flashy like the Alpha Girls, but each had their own quiet kind of beauty.

Up until now, all the four-person groups had already partnered with everyone inside their circles.

But by teaming up again, the remaining Alpha and Beta Girls could swap partners within their groups, which meant they could probably last at least four more rounds.

It was painfully clear that the smaller, weaker third-tier Groundling girls would be the next to fall.

Hime watched Lara's sharply handsome profile – the kind that could have landed her a lead role at the Takarazuka Revue – then took a deep breath, made up her mind and stepped away from the huddle of third-tier girls to return to her desk.

Wasn't it 'cause you wanted to be someone else for a while?

As Emi's words echoed in her mind, Hime pulled a pair of scissors from her floral pencil case and walked back toward the others.

'. . . Hime? What are you doing?' Seeing the scissors in Hime's hand, Umi looked at her like she had lost her mind.

'There's something I've always wanted to be,' Hime said, bringing the blades close to her face. 'I wanted to be a prince.'

With one decisive snip after another, she cut her hair – once long and beautiful enough that Karen had complimented it – into a short, jagged crop.

Yes. Back then, Hime had never wanted to be Snow White. She had wanted to be the prince.

She had joined the drama club not because she loved acting, but because she had hoped she might get to play a male role.

All her life, Hime had felt out of place in her own skin as a girl. But she had never told anyone – not even her best friend, Emi. Partly out of fear that people would find her disgusting, but also because the very idea of wanting to be a boy felt taboo.

Her mother, even past forty, was obsessed – almost manically – with the kind of pink, frilly toys little girls collected. She even claimed to have married Hime's father just because she wanted the surname Shirayuki. According to her dad, when she found out she was pregnant, she had thrown a fit, saying she would get an abortion if the baby wasn't a girl. Since she got her wish, she insisted the child had to be named Hime – written as *Sunshine Bud*, but not coincidentally pronounced the same as *Princess* – to make her a real-life Snow White.

So, when Hime was cast as Snow White in the elementary school play, her mother had been overjoyed.

Yet it wasn't long until that joy turned into fury.

Hime had cut her hair short for the role. She had always kept it long because her mother demanded it, but she thought Snow White should have short hair. That was all.

'Hime, why would you cut your hair like that when you finally get to play Snow White? It looks awful! You're already plain-looking, short hair just makes it worse! Don't you get it? You're unattractive, so at least try to *look* feminine!'

Her mother would cry and curse her every time she looked at her hair. It didn't matter how often Hime insisted that Snow White had short hair.

'Listen, Hime. If you ever do something like this again, I really *will* throw you out of this house, do you hear me? You were lucky enough to be born a girl, so even if you *are* ugly, live cute, okay?'

All Hime could do was nod. She had been made to swear to *live like a girl*. Ever since, she had obeyed that command – took care of her hair, let it grow long again – so it wasn't surprising that Karen had praised it.

Once she entered middle school, her mother started buying her floral-patterned things – clothes, underwear, bedding, even her pencil case. Her mother was extreme that way. Somehow, she had decided that floral prints suited Hime perfectly.

'Wow, it's so pretty. Thanks, Mum.'

Every time, Hime pretended to be happy. She had to. Her mother's gifts weren't born from cruelty, but from love.

Even though, deep down, she never wanted to see another flower again.

'Hime, stop!' Umi screamed, her face turning pale. She was standing on the flower petals scattered from the chest of someone already disqualified.

It was the first time Hime had seen her raise her voice like that outside of acting practice.

But Hime watched her calmly, like it was happening to someone else.

Why? Because she had just torn off her own corsage.

If she was going to die sooner or later anyway, then she wanted, at least at the end, to die as herself.

Hime took one last deep breath, smiled under the fluorescent lights and looked down at Umi.

'Hey, Umi, if you're still alive at the end . . . could you tell Emi something for me?'

Sorry I said you couldn't make it.

She had only said it out of jealousy – because she hadn't wanted Emi to leave.

She had always admired Emi, who was never pretty, nor the best actress, but who always stood tall and believed in herself.

Hey, Emi . . . If we're reborn someday, will you be my friend again?

Round 4

<u>Standby:</u> Mishin Mizushima

Sarasa Hoshikawa - Yu Nikaido
Urin Nekoya - Yuki Koiwai
Lisa Okami - Katsune Nakano
Lara Kagahi - Leika Tomoe
Karen Asakura - Kiko Masugi
Lutsu Kanamori - Yayoi Yoitani
Nodoka Saeki - Sayuki Sena
Nichika Saeki -
Uta Marguerite Samejima
Natsuki Himuro - Sui Inoue
Setsuna Kuroki - Inori Rokujo
Moe Fuyuno - Umi Hagiwara

Disqualified:
Hime Shirayuki

Students Remaining: 23

Time Left:
39 minutes

Chapter 5: Your Worth
Moe Fuyuno

It was no wonder people were losing their minds, Moe thought to herself.

The fourth round had ended when Hime Shirayuki had pulled off her own corsage and essentially blown herself up.

Her body looked like some grotesque kind of art – or maybe a trashy doll. Her uniform was covered in full-bloom roses of every colour.

Moe figured the cause of death was the thorns piercing her skin, the poison spreading through her body. She had no idea how it worked, but the idea that removing your own corsage could do that made her shudder.

Trying to look away from the growing pile of strange corpses, she glanced at the clock. It read 9:21. Thirty-nine minutes left. Twenty-three students still alive.

Was she the only one watching all this with a kind of detached fascination? Maybe she really was insane. Moe looked down at the worn toes of her loafers and gave a bitter little laugh.

The number was odd this time, so no one had to wait the round out.

Before Lutsu Kanamori – the de facto organizer by now – could even speak, the Alpha and Beta Girls were already pairing off within their merged groups, swapping partners as planned.

'Who do you think will get disqualified this time?'

'This is way too scary . . .'

Maybe the relief of knowing they were safe for a few more rounds had emboldened them. To Moe, it looked like they were pretending to be scared while actually enjoying watching the doomed third-tier girls squirm.

People at the top always got their kicks watching the misery of those at the bottom. Deep down, they were probably thinking, *Come on, Groundlings, just hurry up and die.* Even if that poison would eventually come back to choke them, they couldn't help it.

This world really was full of idiots.

But that couldn't be helped. Even facing death, no one wanted to hold hands with someone from a lower group. Moe had known that long before this game started.

That was why, when Aoi Morita from the Beta Girls had died earlier, Moe had felt nothing but relief. When Aoi had asked her to pair up, Moe had honestly wanted to kill her. The nerve – to suddenly act like they were friends, after spending so much time looking down on her.

To Moe, someone that hopelessly self-centred didn't deserve to live. If a girl like that survived, she would only go on to waste her life – marry some loser, post about her parenting on Instagram and think she was special.

'Hey . . . Looks like one of us is gonna die next,' Umi Hagiwara said, loosening her grip.

Their hands had been locked so tightly their palms were damp with each other's sweat.

Moe nodded. It was a fair assessment.

Last round, Natsuki Himuro had paired with Sui Inoue, and Setsuna Kuroki had paired with Inori Rokujo – which meant the four could just swap partners one more time. No one else would risk leaving their groups to find someone new.

That meant either she or Umi would inevitably end up with Mishin Mizushima – the *designated student* – and one of them would be left over.

Last round, Moe had been the one to reach out first and take Umi's hand.

The reason was simple – she wanted Umi to live.

'Hagiwara,' she said, looking straight at her. 'You should be the one to get out of this alive.'

'Huh?'

'I know your worth.'

There were, after all, two kinds of people in this world – those who understood literature, and those who didn't even try.

Moe remembered Tweeting that on her book-lover account the night before, smiling faintly as she addressed Umi.

She had always liked reading, but she only truly fell in love with it in the summer of her second year in middle school. For her book report, she had checked out *The Wind-Up Bird Chronicle* by Haruki Murakami from the library – the original version, in three thick volumes. She thought it would keep her busy all vacation.

It was *surreal* – maybe that was the word. Hard to grasp at that age. She couldn't fully understand what the story meant, but while she was reading, she felt like she wasn't in this world anymore – like dreaming while still awake. By the time she finished, after about a month, she felt like she had shed a layer of skin and stepped into another dimension.

After that, she devoured Murakami's novels like an addict. Every time she finished one, it felt like she was peeling away her own immaturity, layer by layer. But by the time she graduated middle school, even Murakami's prose had lost that power to transport her.

She had wanted to find that feeling again – the kind of writing that could take her somewhere else.

When she finally did, it came from the place she had least expected – a two-person play at the school culture festival in her second year of high school.

The play was called *Zinnia*.

Nobody was paying attention – after all, the cast was made up entirely of third-tier girls. The audience, seniors and juniors alike, snickered at Emi Akanishi, the class's designated *ugly girl* who had the nerve to act with confidence.

But Moe was transfixed. She thought anyone who couldn't see how good it was had to be an idiot.

To be honest, Emi's acting was passable, but Hime Shirayuki's was so awkward it was almost painful to watch. She probably didn't even understand what her lines meant.

But the script, written by Umi Hagiwara, the president of the drama club, was razor-sharp – breathtakingly so.

Zinnia captured the undying longing for a vanished friend with words only she could have written – lines the likes of which Moe had never experienced before.

It was hard to believe a classmate had written it. Moe was sure Umi would become a great writer someday – and the realization crushed her.

Ever since discovering Murakami, Moe had been writing little stories of her own, between classes, before bed.

But they were laughably bad.

Even in a hundred years, she would never be Murakami. And after watching that play, she knew she would never be Umi Hagiwara, either.

Seeing that script forced her to admit it – she was ordinary. A nobody who could only ever adore genius from afar.

'Your play was amazing, Hagiwara,' she had told her three days later, still riding the high. 'Was it for Shirayuki? Because Akanishi left? I looked up what zinnia flowers symbolize – mourning an absent friend, thoughts of a friend who's gone – and it all made sense. The more I thought about it, the deeper it got. Honestly, the acting was . . . yeah, not great. But the script – it was incredible. I haven't felt that kind of trip into another world in forever. Thank you.'

She had spoken too fast, tripping over her words, and Umi had just stared at her, speechless.

They were both quiet girls, both in the third tier, and they had barely spoken before. Her reaction made sense. Still, Moe had been sure she was happy. Writing had to be her whole identity.

'Anyway, just remember – I'm your fan now,' Moe had said before walking away.

That day, she decided she would be proud to call herself Umi Hagiwara's most dedicated reader.

Even if she couldn't write, she could read and she could see. That, she believed, was her only real talent.

Now, she found herself saying, fast and breathless again, 'I know I've said it before, Hagiwara, but I'm your fan. It probably makes no sense, but you're my dream. So, you've got to become someone great. You've got to live. To the end. And become a real writer.'

She meant it – but she was also half-delirious. Even a Murakami protagonist wouldn't have the nerve to mutter to himself in exasperation in a situation like this.

'. . . Got it,' Umi said, nodding.

She probably didn't understand at all. The only thing they both understood was that whichever of them died in this round, neither of them would make it to the end.

That was why Moe knew she could sacrifice herself.

She just wanted Umi to know that she was the more valuable of the two. That was the only mission she had left.

'I'll be cheering for you even after I'm dead,' Moe said with a smile that didn't really suit her.

'. . . Thank you.' After a small pause, Umi smiled back, and Moe nearly burst into tears.

In this classroom, talent meant nothing. Surrounded by people who didn't even try to understand literature, Umi was labelled a Groundling girl. But Moe knew better – she knew that Umi had more worth than any of the pretty Alpha Girls or the bland Beta ones.

Round 5

Sarasa Hoshikawa - Yuki Koiwai
Urin Nekoya - Leika Tomoe
Lisa Okami - Yu Nikaido
Lara Kagahi - Katsune Nakano
Karen Asakura - Sayuki Sena
Lutsu Kanamori -
Uta Marguerite Samejima
Nodoka Saeki - Yayoi Yoitani
Nichika Saeki - Kiko Masugi
Setsuna Kuroki - Sui Inoue
Natsuki Himuro - Inori Rokujo
Mishin Mizushima - Umi Hagiwara

Disqualified:
Moe Fuyuno

Students Remaining: 22

Time Left:
37 minutes

Chapter 6: I'm . . . Alive
Natsuki Himuro

Moe Fuyuno, now disqualified, had been torn apart by knives shaped like flower petals, scattering in rhythm with the death countdown. Her body, dyed a deep red, reminded Natsuki of the red cover of a novel Moe had once recommended – a book she had found unbearably dull.

As the reflection of Moe's ruined body flickered in her narrow, crescent-moon eyes, all Natsuki could do was despair. She had already joined hands with Umi Hagiwara, who had survived, but she could have paired with Moe, too. Since Umi had no one else left to partner with anyway, Natsuki couldn't help but wish Moe had been spared instead.

- You cannot pair with the same person twice.

Because of that rule, after pairing with Inori Rokujo and Sui Inoue – who had been left out of the Beta Girls group – there was no one else left who could partner with her.

Surrounded by corpses that grew bloodier by the minute, tears began to spill down her cheeks.

The Alpha Girls, Beta Girls A and B and the student council were each made up of four people. Since the previous rounds, they had merged into two larger groups of eight. Those girls wouldn't need to look for new partners for at least two more rounds.

'Setsuna . . . I'm scared.'

Without thinking, Natsuki threw herself against Setsuna Kuroki, who stood silently beside her.

For Natsuki, who had lost her entire family in an accident, her best friend Setsuna was the only support she had left in this world.

'It's okay, Natsuki.' Setsuna wrapped her trembling body in her arms and patted her gently on the back.

'How is any of this okay? We're finished. We're . . . We're going to die.'

Setsuna cupped Natsuki's cool, pale cheeks between her still-warm hands and spoke in a steady, almost serene voice that gave no hint she might soon be disqualified. 'Natsuki, calm down. We're the chosen ones. Dying? That's not going to happen.'

'No . . . We're dying *because* we weren't chosen . . .' Her words came out slurred as Setsuna's hands pressed against her cheeks.

'. . . Hey. Even if that's true, Natsuki, I'm not afraid. Not at all.'

Setsuna smiled – a bright, dazzling smile completely at odds with her status as a so-called Groundling. Now that Natsuki thought about it, Setsuna had always been like that.

Setsuna had come to the children's home where Natsuki lived near the end of their first spring in high school.

Since they attended the same school, the staff decided to put them in the same room. At school, though, they hadn't been close friends – just classmates.

That first night, Natsuki felt restless and couldn't sleep. She had always had a room to herself, and the presence of another person made it impossible to relax. Besides, even if Setsuna was a bit of an oddball, she was stunningly beautiful – so much so that Natsuki couldn't help but compare herself to her.

'Hey, since we're going to be roommates from now on, why don't we tell each other about ourselves?'

It was two in the morning when Setsuna, who also couldn't sleep, sat up and made the suggestion.

'Okay,' Natsuki agreed. It felt like the right thing to do.

Driven by a shared urge to better familiarize themselves with each other, they talked breathlessly, barely pausing for air. Favourite colours, favourite weather, favourite foods, manga, music, celebrities – and finally, just before dawn, Setsuna brought up something else.

'You know, I've actually almost died a bunch of times. My parents used to hold me under bathwater full of weird-coloured bath salts, or leave me out on the balcony in the snow for hours. Sometimes, they wouldn't feed me for days, or they'd hit and kick me every day. But somehow, I never died. Crazy, right?'

She told the story of her parents' abuse like it was nothing more than a humorous anecdote.

'How could anyone do something that awful to their own child . . .? I can't believe it.'

Maybe it was just bravado on Setsuna's part, but Natsuki couldn't stop crying, even though Setsuna herself sounded so casual about it. Maybe it was because they had been talking all night that her emotions were wound tight, or maybe it was because she had grown up in a warm, loving family that made it impossible to comprehend Setsuna's world.

'Don't cry, Natsuki. But thank you . . . I used to think it was normal, that all parents were like that. When they got arrested, I didn't understand what was happening. Even now, everyone here is so kind, it still feels strange. You crying for me – that's strange, too. I guess it's because your parents loved you, right?'

Natsuki nodded, wiping her tears with the sleeve of her polka-dotted GU pyjamas, and said in a hoarse whisper, 'But they died because of me.'

She had never told any of her classmates that. She had never dared to.

But for some reason, she wanted Setsuna to know what she had done.

Just as Setsuna guessed, Natsuki had lived surrounded by her parents' love before coming to the children's home.

Her mother's cakes were the best in the world, and her father's big, gentle hand could scoop away all the sadness she brought home from school. Their house was always full of laughter. Natsuki could remember every detail – the painting of yellow flowers by the entryway, the spotless living room, the cozy wooden bedroom where they all slept together. The staff at the home were kind, and she was grateful. But if she could have chosen, she would have stayed in that sunlit house forever.

Everything had ended during the summer vacation of her second year of middle school.

It had been a warm day – the day of the Lake Biwa Great Fireworks Festival, a family tradition since she was small. No matter how crowded it got, they always went together. To Natsuki, summer meant fireworks even more than watermelon or swimming pools.

That year, the festival went as smoothly as it ever did. No matter how many times she saw them, the fireworks always stirred her heart.

'Alright, shall we head home?'

Just before the finale began, her father stood up. They always left before the end to avoid the traffic jam getting out of the parking lot.

But that night, Natsuki tugged on his beige pants and said she wanted to see the finale – just once, up close.

'Well, I guess getting stuck in traffic once in a while is part of the fun.'

'That's right. Let's stay till the end.'

Maybe because she almost never asked for anything, her parents agreed right away.

But it was a mistake.

If they had left early as usual, that terrible accident would never have happened.

After the finale ended, the crowd began to surge all at once. The streets were so packed they could barely move.

'The parking lot's probably a mess right now. Let's wait a bit – sit by the lake and talk for a while,' her father suggested.

They spent about an hour by Lake Biwa, chatting while the night breeze cooled their faces. Though as vast as the sea, the lake was calm, without waves. Smoke from the fireworks still lingered in the sky.

When the crowds finally thinned, they headed back to the car.

'Thanks to you, Natsuki, we got to see such an amazing finale. I think we've been missing out all these years,' her father said, flashing a smile in the rearview mirror as he started the engine.

'Yeah. Thanks for bringing us again this year. Next year, let's all –'

Go again.

She never finished the sentence.

A group of drunk college boys suddenly stumbled onto the road.

Natsuki couldn't see everything from the back seat, but her father must have swerved to avoid them – instinctively.

That movement led straight to the crash.

In the oncoming lane was a massive delivery truck. The impact crushed the front of their car like an empty can. Her father and mother were killed instantly.

She was the only one who survived.

After that lonely summer that felt like sinking to the bottom of the sea, with no relatives to rely on, Natsuki was sent to the children's home.

'Ever since that day, I've wanted to die. But I can't. I'm too scared to die. Even though I was the only one who lived . . . It's pathetic, right?'

By the time she finished talking, her face was a mess of tears and snot.

'. . . I'm not scared of dying,' Setsuna said.

Her voice felt like a cold raindrop landing on the tip of Natsuki's nose after the rain had stopped.

'Why not?'

'Well . . . There's a magic spell that takes away your fear of dying. I'll teach it to you – just for you.'

Magic. It had been a long time since Natsuki had heard that word, one she used to love as a child.

'Hold out your right index finger.'

'Okay.'

She did as she was told.

Setsuna pulled a utility knife from the drawer beside her bed.

'What are you doing?'

Seeing the sharp blade made Natsuki hesitate. The word *wrist-cutting* – something she had only ever read in manga – flashed through her mind.

'It's fine. Just close your eyes.'

Still, she didn't resist. Her brain was foggy with exhaustion, and part of her wanted – needed – the magic Setsuna was offering.

'Alright, here comes the spell.'

Natsuki grimaced as a stinging pain shot through her fingertip. She couldn't see what was happening, but she could guess.

'You can open your eyes now.'

When she did, her index finger was bleeding, a thin red line split open across it. The colour reminded her of the sashimi they had eaten for dinner.

Then, Setsuna did the same to her own finger.

'The magic starts now. Natsuki, point your finger toward mine.'

Natsuki did as she was told. A drop of blood fell onto her mattress.

Setsuna pressed her fingertip to Natsuki's.

The sight reminded Natsuki of something – yes, the poster for *E.T.*, the movie her parents had loved to watch with her.

Just as she remembered the title, Setsuna spoke.

'I'm . . . alive,' she said in the same halting tone E.T. used in the movie.

'That's the spell. Say it, Natsuki.'

'Yeah.'

Natsuki almost laughed. It was obvious Setsuna had just made it up for her. But even if it wasn't real, it still made her happy.

Their fingers touched. They looked at each other and whispered the words together: 'I'm . . . alive.'

Unable to bear the stench of blood any longer, Natsuki quietly opened one of the windows.

In that instant, the sound of the pouring rain became crystal clear.

'. . . Since we have an even number this time, we'll need to decide who will sit out. Anyone voting for Mishin Mizushima, please raise your hand.'

With each round, the odds of surviving grew slimmer. When Lutsu Kanamori called out to the room in her hesitant voice, everyone except Mishin herself and Lisa Okami from the Alpha Girls' group raised their hands.

If they chose anyone but Mishin, chaos would break out. And if the votes split, it would just waste time. On top of that, if the *designated student* ended up without a partner, everyone else would be disqualified. With that rule in place, it was safest to have Mishin sit out.

'In that case, the student sitting out this round will be Mizushima.'

The moment the decision was made, classmates all over the room began joining hands.

Natsuki clung to Setsuna, unable to face what was happening any longer. Averting her gaze was the only way she could keep her fear from overwhelming her.

'Hey, wait a second! *I* don't have anyone to pair with!' Lisa Okami's angry shout echoed through the room.

After combining with Beta Girls B the round before last, each of the Alpha Girls should, by calculation, have had two more rounds before they would need to find new partners.

Natsuki cautiously looked up toward the commotion.

Sarasa Hoshikawa was paired with Leika Tomoe.

Urin Nekoya was with Katsune Nakano.

Lara Kagahi was holding hands with Yuki Koiwai.

That left Yu Nikaido. And yet . . .

'Hey. I already paired up with Yu earlier. What the hell?'

To be honest, Natsuki couldn't remember who had paired with whom anymore. But if Lisa said that was how it was, then that probably *was* how it was.

'Oh, right, right. Guess we messed up the order of the pairing. Didn't think that far ahead. Sorry, Lisa-Lisa!' Urin chuckled, fixing her with a grin.

Acting on impulse, Lisa grabbed Urin by the collar with her bracelet-covered arm. 'What? You *didn't think that far ahead*? Are you trying to get me killed here?'

Instead of backing down, Urin tilted her head up and goaded her with a smug smile. 'Well, *you* didn't think that far ahead, either, Lisa-Lisa. And if you don't find someone soon, you're going to get left out, you know?'

Sure, Lisa was partly to blame for not thinking, but she must have realized there was no time left for arguing. She let Urin go, kicked the nearest chair out of frustration and scanned the room.

For a brief moment, Natsuki thought she saw a glimmer of hope as Lisa's eyes met hers.

But that light vanished just as quickly. As if to make clear that a Groundling like Natsuki didn't so much as exist in her world, Lisa turned away and walked right past her. Then, she grabbed Sui Inoue's hand – Sui, who was standing there just as lost as she was – and forced the pair together.

'Yu, you go with Inori,' she tossed out triumphantly to Yu, who had been left without a partner in the Beta Girls B group.

Following Lisa's instruction, Yu quickly reached for the hand of Inori Rokujo, Sui's partner.

Meanwhile, the rest of the Beta Girls B group and the student council members seemed to have planned their pairings carefully. There was no commotion among them.

In other words, this round would wipe out every third-tier girl except for Mishin.

Umi must have known she wouldn't make it through this round. She had given up on finding a partner from the start and sat quietly at her desk, writing something. Whether it was a will or a script, Natsuki had no time left to find out.

'It's okay, Natsuki.' Setsuna, trembling so hard her teeth chattered like the shivering emoji she often used in LINE, wrapped her arms around her and tried to comfort her. 'Dying isn't scary. Because when we're reborn, we'll definitely be happier than we are now. A new, wonderful life will begin. We've been chosen for that.'

Maybe Setsuna had lived her whole life wanting to be reborn as someone else. But Natsuki didn't feel that way. She wanted to be reborn as herself again – to be born once more to those wonderful parents she had lost.

Petal by petal, with merciless tiny blips, the flowers on their chests began to fall away.

'I'm scared . . . I'm really scared . . .'

That was all Natsuki could say at this point.

'Well, I guess it can't be helped. I'll make an exception and cast the spell one more time,' Setsuna said with innocent cheer as she pulled a box cutter from her skirt pocket.

It was hard to imagine she kept such a thing on her all the time, so Natsuki understood – Setsuna had brought it just for this, to cast this spell.

Setsuna took Natsuki's hand and, without hesitation, sliced open her fingertip. Then, she did the same to herself.

Their bleeding fingers touched, like in *E.T.*

'Remember the magic words?' Setsuna asked.

Just as the last petal fell, Natsuki nodded.

'I'm . . . alive.'

Round 6

Standby: Mishin Mizushima

Sarasa Hoshikawa - Leika Tomoe
Urin Nekoya - Katsune Nakano
Lisa Okami - Sui Inoue
Lara Kagahi - Yuki Koiwai
Karen Asakura -
Uta Marguerite Samejima
Lutsu Kanamori - Sayuki Sena
Nichika Saeki - Yayoi Yoitani
Nodoka Saeki - Kiko Masugi
Yu Nikaido - Inori Rokujo

Disqualified:
Umi Hagiwara
Natsuki Himuro
Setsuna Kuroki

Students Remaining: 19

Time Left:
33 minutes

Chapter 7: Hated by Life Itself
Inori Rokujo

Inori was barely able to breathe.

She couldn't stop trembling. The terror made it painfully real – this game killed those who had no friends.

Last time, three girls had been disqualified all at once, all of them Groundlings. They had simply run out of people willing to team up with them.

Umi Hagiwara still sat at her desk, clutching her pen, frozen in place. Natsuki Himuro and Setsuna Kuroki were locked in an embrace, motionless, as if turned to ice.

Who could have created such a cursed, evil sort of corsage? What kind of mechanism was hidden inside her own – and how would it kill her when her time came?

'Sui . . .' Clutching at the name like a spider's thread, Inori met Sui Inoue's eyes.

'Inori . . .' Sui called back, her voice was worn to exhaustion.

The student who would die this round had already been decided before the game even began.

It was either her or Sui.

And the one to die next, too, would be her or Sui.

It was now only a matter of who went first.

But truthfully, just like the Groundlings, they both should have already been disqualified. During the last round, when the Alpha Girls and the upper Beta Girls paired off, the order had been random. Inori had been lucky enough to hold hands with Yu, and Sui with Lisa – both Alpha Girls – and that luck had saved them.

Inori took a deep breath, then finally forced herself to look toward the place she had been avoiding all this time – Aoi Morita's body.

The corsage had burrowed deep into her chest. The pain

must have been excruciating, rendering her once-lovely face unrecognizable.

Time had lost all meaning to her, but Aoi's disqualification had been only ten minutes ago.

Inori quietly stepped closer, trembling as she pressed her hands together in prayer.

She was truly grateful to Aoi.

As her bandmate, Aoi had pulled her and Sui – two awkward, nerdy girls – from the depths of the third-tier group and made them into something like normal high schoolers. When Lisa Okami chose them over the Groundlings earlier, Inori had felt in her bones what that difference meant. And she knew all too well how small that difference really was. In a few minutes, she and Sui would be dead, too. But right now, those few minutes felt infinitely precious.

How much did Aoi resent them, dying without a chance to prepare herself?

'You'll both be dead soon anyway!'

What had she been feeling when she screamed those words?

Maybe she had felt betrayed by them, Inori thought.

'. . . I'm the worst.'

She had every right to curse them.

Because when Aoi's disqualification was announced, the first feeling that rose in Inori's chest hadn't been grief. It had been relief. And the second – a faint, shameful hope that maybe she and Sui could survive together.

Just as Moe Fuyuno had accused her, Aoi hadn't been without selfishness. And Inori had known that Aoi sometimes looked down on them. But her failure to feel grief wasn't because she had hated Aoi. Neither she nor Sui had ever spoken ill of her. In fact, they had liked her. She was bright, funny, caring, hardworking. She probably never actually liked Vocaloid music, yet she had humoured their interests, and had even played their favourite songs for the culture festival.

They had spent three years together in the light music club – a lifetime's worth of memories.

And it wasn't just at club after school. At lunch, they had always gathered at Aoi's desk, and on the way home, they would stop by the Jeugia store in Shinkyogoku, just like a proper light music club. Sometimes, they would sing karaoke at Sanjo-Kawaramachi, eat parfaits at Karafuneya, take photobooth pictures at Round One. Without question, their time together had been the stuff of youth itself.

Inori moved closer to Aoi's body and gently laid a pale blue handkerchief over her distorted face. As if in silent understanding, Sui likewise rushed over, covering Aoi's chest – where the corsage had dug its way into her – with a pink handkerchief.

Both handkerchiefs had little embroidered cats on them. They had been Christmas presents from Aoi.

'We'll all match,' she had said, showing them her yellow one with the same design.

Only now did the grief catch up to Inori, burning at the corners of her eyes.

'I'm sorry, Aoi . . . I'm so sorry.'

This time, she couldn't hold the words back.

When she glanced beside her, Sui was crying silently, too.

Inori knew – Sui had always felt the same way she did about their trio.

Being in a group of three had, in a way, been easy.

They just had to follow behind Aoi, listen to her talk and nod along like characters in an RPG. It wasn't meant as an insult – for two girls who were bad at asserting themselves, having someone to lead the way had been a blessing.

Inori's reason for joining the light music club had partly been Aoi's obsession with the anime *K-On!*, which had aired while they were still in elementary school.

Her true reason for wanting to make music, however, came later, when she discovered the incredible songs made by Vocaloid producers online. Each god-tier track she found made flowers bloom in her once-empty life. She dreamed of one day posting her own *sang it* or *played it* videos.

So, when Aoi volunteered to play drums, Inori's heart leapt. Guitar dominated the *played it* scene, and even for *sang it* videos, being able to play guitar made you look that much cooler.

But when Sui said, 'I'll play bass,' Inori immediately knew it wasn't just to let her have guitar and vocals. She had seen the charm hanging from Sui's school bag – merchandise from a Vocaloid producer they both liked, one who was also a famous, handsome bassist.

Though they followed different creators, their shared love of the Vocaloid world quickly deepened their friendship. Before long, they were best friends. Talking about music with someone who truly *understood* – that was something that made Inori genuinely happy.

But they were a trio. Spending time together without Aoi felt like a betrayal.

'Hey, Sui, let's do that thing today.'

'Yeah.'

And so, *that thing* became their secret ritual.

They would share a single pair of wireless earbuds, each wearing one, and secretly listen to songs during class – one of them choosing the tracks each time.

A few times a month, on days when the teachers were lax, they would play this game – taking turns every period, like a music exchange. They kept updating their playlists, ready for whenever the opportunity presented itself.

Then, at lunch or after school – when Aoi went to the bathroom – they would quietly trade their thoughts. Those whispered conversations were their favourite moments.

'Hey, Sui, which song did you like best today?'

'"Butterfly on My Right Shoulder", I think.'

'Knew you'd say that.'

'And that Chouchou-P medley – amazing.'

'Right? Chouchou-P will always be god-level.'

'How about mine?'

'"Karakuri Pierrot" was great, and Hachi's "Dune", too.'

'You always get me, Sui. I thought Hachi would never write another Hatsune Miku song, so "Dune" hit hard.'

'Yeah, he's totally Kenshi Yonezu now.'

'Well, Yonezu's a god, as well.'

'Because he was Hachi first.'

When Aoi wasn't around – when it was just the two of them – Inori finally felt like she could talk as herself. She was sure Sui felt the same.

Sometimes, deep down, she caught herself wishing Aoi would never come back from the bathroom.

'No one will have to sit this round out,' Lutsu Kanamori, standing at the teacher's desk like an instructor, announced.

Inori vaguely wondered who would take over the role after Lutsu herself was disqualified. Absentmindedly, she took her wireless earbuds from her blazer pocket.

'. . . Sui, let's do that thing one last time.'

Like always, she held out one earbud to her.

Her hand was trembling.

She had never realized how terrifying death could be, even though so many of the songs she loved were filled with it. She had only thought she understood what it meant to *want* to die – or to want to live.

'For the last song . . . can I choose?' Sui's voice shook as she took the earbud.

'Yeah,' Inori nodded, fitting hers in place.

Whichever one chose, it would have been the same song anyway – and sure enough, a few seconds later, the intro that filled her ears was the one she loved most.

How many times had they played that melody, sharing it in their hearts? They looked at each other and nodded. Then, they stepped forward together, toward Mishin Mizushima, and held out their hands.

Inori thought that the two of them probably looked more like ghosts than the girl who was always being called one in the class LINE group.

'Mizushima, could you take one of our hands?'

When she listened to music, Inori always felt like she was invincible, the hero of the world. That false courage gave her the strength to speak up now.

Mishin looked terrified. Inori knew she was asking something cruel. But they couldn't choose who would die first themselves.

'There's no time. Hurry up and pick,' came Lisa Okami's snarky voice from behind.

Inori closed her eyes. She was sure Sui did, too.

Now, the same song, 'Hated by Life Itself', played in both their ears. No matter who was chosen, no matter whose flower fell first, their hearts would remain connected.

Round 7

Sarasa Hoshikawa - Kiko Masugi
Urin Nekoya -
Uta Marguerite Samejima
Lisa Okami - Yayoi Yoitani
Lara Kagahi - Sayuki Sena
Lutsu Kanamori - Yu Nikaido
Karen Asakura - Yuki Koiwai
Nodoka Saeki - Katsune Nakano
Nichika Saeki - Leika Tomoe
Mishin Mizushima - Inori Rokujo

Disqualified:
Sui Inoue

Students Remaining: 18

Time Left:
29 minutes

Chapter 8: Deserving of Life
Lisa Okami

After Lisa gave the signal, Mishin Mizushima closed her eyes and took Inori Rokujo's hand.

She was probably leaving it to fate, but as far as Lisa was concerned, it didn't matter who she chose. Either way, the one she went with would almost certainly be disqualified in the next round.

Inori seemed to know that, too. She had her wireless earbuds in, listening to music. Her last supper – or rather, her last song.

Lisa's thoughts drifted idly, until a few moments later, Sui Inoue began to convulse, all her petals gone.

Ah, electrocution this time, Lisa thought, resting her chin on her hand as she watched Sui's end.

'Inoue's gone,' she said flatly, stretching her arms and letting out a huge, bored yawn.

'Since it's an even round, we'll now choose a standby student. Please raise your hand if you vote for Mizushima,' announced Lutsu Kanamori as soon as Sui's death was confirmed

With that, the next round began.

Lisa had no idea what gave Lutsu the authority to act like some big shot just because she was a bit of a brain and a former student council president, but ever since the game had begun, she had been bossing everyone around like she ran the place.

It grated on Lisa's nerves. Still, all she could do to rebel was refuse to raise her hand. When the number of players was even, they had to decide on someone to *sit out* each round, and they needed someone to keep the process going.

As usual, every hand went up but hers.

'The standby student will be Mizushima,' Lutsu declared, wearing that same bitter, tight-lipped expression she always did during these announcements.

Lisa tuned her out, thinking to herself, *Why does it always have to be Mizushima, anyway?*

Logically, if everyone took turns waiting out, the odds of forming a pair would go up for everyone. But since the rules said it had to be decided by vote and not rock-paper-scissors, taking turns was basically impossible. The cautious ones always voted for Mishin to make sure the *designated student* didn't get left out. Once things got desperate, everyone would just prioritize themselves or their friends.

Lisa let out a long sigh, loud enough for the whole room to hear.

If everyone would just vote for *her*, things would be so much simpler. Hell, they *should* have been voting for her.

Fed up, she walked over to Lutsu and said, 'Hey, Prez, let's swap the group pairings. Things got all confusing last round, and my head's still scrambled about who I've been with. This way, it'll be easier for everyone to keep track, right?'

Right now, the Alpha Girls were paired with Beta Girls B. Lisa was asking to switch so they would be paired with the Beta Girls A instead – the ones currently teamed with the student council members.

Her suggestion earned nods from the other Alpha Girls.

'. . . Alright,' Lutsu said after a brief pause. 'That makes sense.'

'Are you sure, Lutsu?' asked Karen Asakura, sounding worried.

'Yeah. I think it's better than rotating the same members over and over,' Lutsu replied.

Watching the two of them, Lisa couldn't help feeling a flash of anger. That perfect honour-student face – Lutsu was just trying to make sure she herself survived.

'You know what, Prez? I bet you and Osuzu are in on this together. You're the one who came up with this stupid game, right?' Lisa accused her. 'No wonder it stinks.'

Though Lutsu silently shook her head, her eyes no longer showed the fear they once had toward Lisa – in fact, there was a hint of disdain in them now.

'That look really pisses me off,' Lisa said. 'If you've got something you want to get off your chest, just say it.'

'There's nothing to say.'

'Don't lie. Say it.'

'Lisa, please, calm down. There's no conspiracy. There's no way Lutsu wants to do this! She could die, too, you know!'

Karen stepped in, unable to watch her friend get cornered. And, to be fair, she was right – there was no guarantee Lutsu would survive, either.

'Fine. Prove it, then. From now on, Karen, you lead the game.'

Lisa knew she was just lashing out, but she didn't care.

'. . . Alright,' Karen said with a hesitant nod.

In that instant, Lisa felt her shoulders loosen, and she realized what had really been eating at her – having to dance to the tune of girls she thought beneath her.

There was only one girl in class Lisa could admit was above her – Karen.

A year ago, last autumn, Karen had dropped into her life like a meteor.

A *real* Alpha Girl, joining them all the way from Tokyo.

If someone that beautiful was just a regular high schooler, Lisa thought, then her idol, Nicole Fujita, must be an actual angel in real life.

Ever since middle school, Lisa had secretly dreamed of becoming a *Popteen* model or a TV personality – because, of course, of Nicole Fujita.

She had poured herself into fashion and makeup, strutted through Kawaramachi hoping to be scouted, but no one ever stopped her. There simply weren't any scouts in Kyoto. If she was serious, she should have been walking around Shibuya or Harajuku in Tokyo.

As such, she started working part-time at a cheap yakiniku chain after school, saving money to head to Tokyo and get discovered.

But the day Karen appeared, that dream crumbled like a sandcastle. Lisa realized there was no point walking through Harajuku – Tokyo must be full of girls as polished and gorgeous as

Karen. Nicole Fujita was just one of the few miracles chosen from among them.

'Hey, Lisa-Lisa,' Urin Nekoya whispered, kneading Lisa's shoulders as if to calm her down. 'Aren't you glad we got to swap groups? You don't need to stress so much. We'll be the ones left standing at the end, you know?'

'Obviously,' Lisa said, flashing a smug smile over her shoulder. *You can die first*, she thought.

From the start, Urin hadn't really been a friend – *negative influence* was probably more accurate.

'Hey, don't you think Sarasa's into Lara? She's cute, but she never gets a boyfriend. It's gotta be love, right?'

'Totally.'

'Right? She's definitely gay.'

That was back at the start of their first summer in high school. After classes, the two of them would head to the local Saizeriya almost every day, trash-talking whoever came to mind. That was how their bond grew – through gossip.

'Sure, Lara's hot, all prince-like and whatever, but she doesn't have the equipment, you know? What's the point of dating her?' Lisa griped between bites of spicy chicken.

She couldn't even imagine girls dating each other – it was unthinkable. And maybe she said that partly to hint that she herself wasn't a virgin. She had lost it at fourteen, to a senior everyone agreed was the hottest guy in school. That made her feel older, more womanly, superior to every other girl in class.

'I wonder how girls even do it,' Urin mused.

'No clue. But at this rate, Sarasa's gonna stay a virgin forever.'

'Lara too.'

'For real.'

'Honestly, besides us, this class is full of country bumpkins. Bet they're all virgins.'

'Yeah, pretty much.'

And with that, Urin had subtly declared that she wasn't a virgin, either – that she was on Lisa's level. Back then, Lisa had still seen herself as the one on top.

She had only ended up at Yasaka Girls' High because she had flunked the entrance exam for public school. Urin had, too. They had gone to the same middle school, though back then, they had barely known each other. It was a huge school, with all kinds of cliques – Lisa had hung with the top *gyaru* crowd, while Urin had been in one of the upper Beta Girl groups, the kind of people who were decent but not flashy.

They hadn't really become friends until high school. And even then, Lisa only befriended her because they had come from the same middle school, and because no one else in their class stood out.

She prided herself on the fact that Urin was only seen as an Alpha Girl in this classroom because she had chosen to associate with her.

High school hierarchies were funny things, Lisa knew – they weren't decided by anyone in particular, yet somehow, they always fell into place. It had nothing to do with personality. You either stood out or you didn't. And in Kyoto, being a *gyaru* like Lisa made you stand out whether you wanted to or not.

'Oh, by the way,' Urin said, poking at her baked Milanese-style doria topped with a soft-boiled egg. 'I've started streaming on YouTube.'

'Huh? What? Like, Hikakin-type videos?' Lisa asked, baffled. The idea of Urin pumping out over-the-top, energetic videos like Hikakin was beyond ridiculous.

'No, it's more chill than that.'

'Oh . . . Okay.'

'I'll send you the channel link. You should check it out.'

'Yeah, sure, when I get home.'

Lisa had thought it was stupid. YouTube? Pathetic. There was no way Urin would ever get popular. She was beneath her, after all.

Just like she had expected, when Lisa clicked the link Urin had sent, none of her videos had any views. The only activity came from creepy comments by pervy men – just the kind of pathetic bottom-feeder YouTuber she deserved to be. The ideas were generic, the editing looked amateur and the sound effects felt slapped on at random. *Chill* was too kind – it was *dull*, like watching someone's boring daily routine. It was obvious at first glance that she didn't have a shred of talent.

Honestly, Lisa had laughed at her behind her back.

But then, at the end of that summer, *it* happened.

'Hey, my video just went crazy viral. I'm dying!'

That was the message Urin sent over LINE.

Lisa checked the channel right away. The video Urin had uploaded a week earlier – *A Boring Summer Day in the Life of a High School Girl* – already had two hundred thousand views. Lisa had watched enough beauty channels to know how huge that was. And considering Urin's videos used to barely hit thirty views in a day, it was unbelievable.

The comments section was full of stuff like, 'She's so cute,' 'Weirdly addictive,' 'I love her vibe' and 'I wanna support this girl.' Most of them came from men.

'This is garbage,' Lisa muttered, closing the app.

How pathetic were those guys, getting off on such mindless crap?

'Hey, look at this video,' she said later to her boyfriend, a college student whose apartment she practically lived in all summer. 'It's blowing up for some reason, but isn't it totally boring?'

'Hmm . . . I kinda like it,' he said.

'Oh yeah? Really?'

'Yeah. Guys dig this kind of thing.'

'. . . Hmph.'

Lisa had never really thought about the kind of videos guys liked. She wondered what he would say if she told him that girl was her friend. She didn't, though. Instead, she just replied to Urin's message with a dumb panda sticker that said *Wow!*

It's a one-time fluke, she thought. *Just dumb luck. Nothing impressive about it.*

But after that day, even Urin's old videos – ones that barely had any views – started racking up numbers.

'Lisa-Lisa! Mornin'!'

Ever since then, Urin had gotten way too casual around her. Calling her *Lisa-Lisa*, of all things, was just the start of it. She used to trail behind her like a sidekick, always sucking up and agreeing with everything.

Considering how they used to spend all their time trash-talking people, Lisa couldn't *not* notice how different Urin's attitude had become.

Urin *definitely* looked down on her now.

At their weekly Saizeriya meetups after school, Urin had stopped gossiping about classmates altogether – a clear sign her battlefield had changed. And it showed – her subscriber count was skyrocketing.

Lisa couldn't vent her frustration anywhere. But still, she kept hanging out with Urin.

She had no idea how other people saw them, but between the two of them, their places had flipped completely.

It all became clear the day Lisa vented about her boyfriend like always, and Urin snorted. The reason came out fast enough. Urin had gotten herself a new boyfriend – a hot one.

'Oh, didn't I tell you? Yeah, I'm seeing someone new. He lives in Tokyo, so it's long-distance, but he's totally obsessed with me. We fall asleep on the phone every night. It's only been a month, and we've already run out of things to say!'

As always, she was poking at her go-to Milanese-style doria with the soft-boiled egg on top, babbling about him. Lisa couldn't remember her ever ordering anything else.

'You got any pictures of him?' Lisa asked, halfway through her popcorn shrimp, not sure how to process the sudden brag.

'Not pictures, exactly. He also does YouTube. Here.'

Urin turned her phone around with a smug grin. On the screen was a Korean-style pretty boy who looked like Changmin from TVXQ. He was exactly Lisa's type. His subscriber count read two hundred thousand.

I've got a lot of followers.

Lisa remembered her own boyfriend saying the same thing, bragging about his one thousand Instagram followers – most of whom were just mutual follows. He was a college guy she had met at the barbecue place where she worked. All her boyfriends came from part-time jobs or random pick-ups by the Kamo River. They were all handsome in that college-boy way – older, so they looked about thirty per cent better by default.

'Wow, he's hot,' Lisa said.

'Right?' Urin beamed.

The more she heard about Urin's fancy new life, the more jealousy ate away at her.

Lisa couldn't stand it. Sure, Urin might have been a semi-popular YouTuber now, but it wasn't like she was prettier or had a better body. As her subscriber count climbed, she had started dressing in a crazier fashion, but strip that away and she was just an ordinary nobody.

'Maybe I should start a YouTube channel, too,' Lisa said. If she were a popular YouTuber, *she* would be the one getting chosen – not Urin.

'Wait, really? If you blow up, we should totally collab!' Urin said, half-smiling, still staring at her phone in its pink bunny-eared case.

Lisa wanted to dump her drink – a mix of Calpis and melon soda from the self-serve bar – right over that smug bob haircut. Urin was *definitely* mocking her.

'God, I hope she dies,' Lisa spat under her breath as she walked home alone from Saizeriya.

She couldn't forgive Urin for pretending to be her friend while secretly laughing at her.

The rain outside the classroom was pounding harder and harder, drumming against the windows. Someone had left one open, and rainwater was blowing in.

'But hey,' Lisa said, adding casually, 'if you die first, I'll upload this video for you, so don't worry.'

She turned toward the phone recording them and struck a peace sign by her mouth, just like Nicole Fujita.

'Thanks,' Urin said, flashing a smile at the camera.

It was obvious – they both secretly wanted the other to die first.

Each of them believed she was the one who deserved to survive. There was no missing that Urin felt that way. After all, she was now a YouTuber with three hundred thousand subscribers.

Watching Inori collapse in tears nearby, death near at hand, Lisa was already plotting.

She would use Urin's demise as her ticket into that world – maybe even steal her boyfriend while she was at it.

She might never become Nicole Fujita, but she could sure as hell beat Urin.

And for that, Lisa was going to survive – no matter what it took.

Because obviously, the one who *should* survive, the one who *deserved* to be famous, wasn't Urin.

It was her.

Round 8

Standby: Mishin Mizushima

Sarasa Hoshikawa -
Uta Marguerite Samejima
Urin Nekoya - Kiko Masugi
Lisa Okami - Sayuki Sena
Lara Kagahi - Yayoi Yoitani
Karen Asakura - Yu Nikaido
Lutsu Kanamori - Yuki Koiwai
Nodoka Saeki - Leika Tomoe
Nichika Saeki - Katsune Nakano

Disqualified:
Inori Rokujo

Students Remaining: 17

Time Left:
27 minutes

Chapter 9: Beta Girls
Yuki Koiwai

The already screaming wind began to howl. Maybe this was what people called a spring storm. In any case, the weather was far too perfectly dramatic for this insane situation.

In just thirty-three minutes since the so-called *game* began, ten classmates had already died.

Yuki gasped again at the sight of Inori Rokujo's still-warm body. Like Sui Inoue, who had been disqualified last time, she had died after a fit of violent convulsions.

Up until the last round, the girls in the upper ranks of the Beta Girls – Yuki among them – had felt a certain safety, a quiet belief that they themselves wouldn't die.

That was because who would be disqualified had, more or less, been predetermined.

But from here on, it wouldn't be surprising if it was one of them.

'Next is . . . Let's see, since it's an odd number, no one needs to sit out.'

Karen Asakura was awkwardly managing the game at the teacher's podium, checking the head count as she went.

A moment ago, Lisa Okami had told her to take over.

Considering the time left, it would have been best if Lutsu Kanamori – by far the smartest student in class – had kept running things. But if you started asking yourself why anyone had to obey Lisa in a situation like this, you had already lost. There was only one answer – it was easier to play along. And Yuki doubted she was the only one who thought so. Probably everyone else did, too. After all, students in their halfway status had no right to speak out.

To Yuki, Lisa was like the emperor with no clothes. She didn't know about the Alpha Girls, but among the Beta ones, almost everyone despised Lisa and secretly looked down on her as a loud, trashy girl who went to extremes trying to stand out. That impression had become crystal clear ever since Karen Asakura, a genuine Alpha Girl, had transferred into their class.

But on the surface, everyone still acted respectfully toward Lisa. It was the complete opposite of how they treated Mishin Mizushima, a third-tier outcast regarded as a ghost and ignored by everyone.

In a sense, Mishin stood out, too – everyone in class knew who she was, though only in a bad way. Compared to that, Yuki knew she was a much fainter presence – not unattractive, but unremarkable in every other way, lumped into her social group simply because of her looks.

Indeed, the middle-tier Beta Girls group she belonged to was little more than a dumping ground for students like her.

'Hey, Yuki . . . When do you think this is going to end? I've got a graduation dinner tonight . . .'

The only exception was Leika Tomoe, an airheaded rich girl who, even now, didn't sense the slightest danger to her own life. Yuki could only give her a strained smile.

Leika was, in short, a natural-born ditz. Painfully so. Sometimes, Yuki wondered if she was faking it, but after three years together, she had learned it was just the kind of foolishness that came from being spoiled rotten as a moneyed princess. It was annoying, but that airheadedness was, in a way, what held their group together.

Yuki, Leika, Katsune Nakano and Yu Nikaido.

The four of them had started hanging out simply because each of them had been desperate for a place to belong and wanted friends who weren't embarrassing to be seen with. That was really all there was to it.

Unlike the Beta Girls A group, which had formed out of genuine friendship built in the calligraphy club, theirs was just a loose collection of second-tier girls.

They were always together at school, but there was no real friendship between them. Even within the group, Yuki often felt bored. She couldn't recall any moment when conversation had truly been fun, or when they had shared genuine laughter. Their only real common ground, aside from being averagely attractive, was that none of them were in any clubs or committees. Including herself, every one of them lacked any real personality. Only Leika, the oblivious rich girl, had a strong character – and even then, it wasn't in a good way.

Still, without Leika, no one else could have taken the lead. Whenever the four of them hung out, trying to confirm a friendship that didn't really exist, it was always Leika who did the inviting.

'Don't worry, I'll pay for this!'

And she always did. Yuki had almost never paid for karaoke or food – maybe just the hundred yen for her share of a photobooth print.

'My dad said I can spend up to a hundred thousand yen a month, but there's nothing I really want. I mean, I can get anything I want anyway. So, let's spend it together! Where should we go next? Lipton for tea parfaits?'

She didn't *have* to spend that money, but maybe this was her way of making friends.

'Oh, right. I've got some clothes and bags I don't use anymore – do you guys want to come over after this?'

She hadn't even been that hungry, but prompted by Leika, Yuki ordered the tea parfait at Lipton and finished it. That was when Leika came out with her invitation.

'Seriously? Lucky!' Katsune squealed, eyes shining.

Every once in a while, Leika would give them her old clothes or bags – sometimes even designer brands no high schooler could afford. That was probably the only perk of being in this dull little group.

'This one would look good on you, Yuki.'

When Leika handed her a Dior bag and Yuki slung it over her shoulder, she had felt, for just a moment, like she was someone special – no longer just another Beta Girl.

*

In gym class, Yuki often got paired up with Yu.

To her, Yu was the most average person in the whole Beta Girls B group. She had dyed her hair a light brown because she didn't like her natural black, collected trendy mascot goods, used nothing but mascot stickers on LINE, told endless stories that went nowhere and always talked about people no one in the group had ever met – her colleagues at her part-time job, her little brother. She was, Yuki thought, profoundly boring.

But she knew other groups probably saw her the same way.

'. . . Have you decided what you're doing after graduation, Yu?' Yuki asked casually as they stretched together before class.

'I'm gonna go to a girls' junior college. Don't really have anything I wanna study. My goal is to find a good boyfriend while I'm there and get married right after graduation. I wanna have kids early,' Yu said with a grin.

Yuki was left speechless. That someone could genuinely want such an ordinary life – it amazed her. She even felt a kind of envy that someone could be born so intensely uninteresting.

'What about you, Yuki? What are you gonna do?' Yu asked with no malice at all.

'Um . . . I haven't really decided yet,' Yuki answered honestly. She didn't know what she wanted to be.

But she *did* know she didn't want a life as ordinary as Yu's. Somewhere deep down, she wanted to deny that she was just another background extra in someone else's story.

That didn't mean she had any big dreams – no desire to be an actress or a writer. She didn't have the courage to put herself out there online like Urin Nekoya did. Standing out scared her. She didn't even have much of an urge for attention.

Maybe that was why, despite not being plain-looking, she was so invisible.

Among the girls in their group, Yuki talked the least. She never started conversations. She only smiled politely at Leika's clueless remarks or Yu's meandering stories that she secretly mocked. She was quiet, passive, forgettable.

'Um . . . Yuki Koiwai, can you pair up with Nodoka please?' Nichika Saeki asked right after Inori was disqualified and the game started again.

She could have just asked Yu, who was standing right beside her, but for some reason, she bowed to Yuki instead.

It was the first time in her life Yuki had ever been chosen for anything.

Without hesitation, she took the offered hand.

'Huh? Yuki? Why . . .?'

By pairing with Nodoka, Yuki had condemned Yu to be left alone – and she didn't feel a flicker of guilt.

'. . . I'm sorry.'

'*Sorry*? Because of you, *I'm* the one left out!' Yu shouted, the red ribbon on her uniform swaying as she stomped her foot.

'Yeah, sorry,' Yuki apologized again in the same calm tone.

Inside, however, for the first time, she found Yu interesting. She also found it interesting that she herself felt nothing about Yu's impending death. If she had been able to speak so honestly from the start, maybe she could have enjoyed high school a bit more – even as a boring person.

She still didn't know what she wanted to be, and in the end, she had decided on a junior college like Yu's.

If she survived this and became an adult, no matter where she ended up, she would probably keep living the same kind of life – always someone in the background.

Looking at things from a distance, she didn't think she deserved to survive more than anyone else.

But even so, Yuki wanted to live.

Round 9

Sarasa Hoshikawa - Yayoi Yoitani
Urin Nekoya - Sayuki Sena
Lisa Okami - Kiko Masugi
Lara Kagahi -
Uta Marguerite Samejima
Karen Asakura - Leika Tomoe
Lutsu Kanamori - Katsune Nakano
Nodoka Saeki - Yuki Koiwai
Nichika Saeki - Mishin Mizushima

Disqualified:
Yu Nikaido

Students Remaining: 16

Time Left:
24 minutes

Chapter 10: Half
Nichika Saeki

Ever since they were little, Nodoka had been helpless without her. She was easily frightened – so much so that even the Haunted Mansion at Disneyland had made her burst into tears.

'It's okay, Nodoka. I'm right here,' Nichika said, rubbing her sister's back to calm her down.

Since before this terrible class started, when Lisa Okami confronted her and she realized that Mr Akiyama, who had collapsed in front of her, had actually died, Nodoka hadn't spoken a single word. The sights that followed after the game began had only made things worse. Both her body and mind had deteriorated instead of recovering. She had only managed to survive this long because Nichika had guided her through it.

The last round, when Yu Nikaido was disqualified, it had been because Nichika asked Yuki Koiwai to hold hands with Nodoka. She hadn't been choosing who to sacrifice – it could have been Yu or Yuki, either one. As long as Nodoka didn't die, that was all that mattered.

Turning away from Yu's body – collapsed, a trickle of blood on her lips, the most ordinary death they had seen so far – Nichika looked up at the ceiling.

And she realized something terrifying.

She was probably the only one who had.

Last time, she had been paired with Mishin Mizushima. She couldn't let Nodoka pair with Mishin, because Mishin was the *designated student*. The rules said that if she was disqualified, everyone else would die. Only two would be left alive. And you couldn't hold hands with the same person twice.

That meant that by the time she had taken Mishin's hand, Nichika had already lost any chance of surviving.

In other words, there was no pathway left for her to live.

And Nodoka still hadn't realized that.

The chance of being born twins was around one per cent.

Out of a hundred pregnancies, one would result in twins. For identical twins, the odds were even lower – zero-point-four per cent.

In other words, Nichika and Nodoka had been born out of a four-in-a-thousand chance.

'Being twins is fun, huh? It's like living twice.'

Nodoka had always found joy in being a twin.

'Yeah,' Nichika would say, smiling back with the same face – but inside, she felt differently.

For as long as she could remember, being a twin had been a cause of grief. She wasn't the only version of herself in the world.

'Nichika, Nodoka – I bought some clothes for you!'

Their mother had been proud of having twin daughters. Maybe she was still riding the high after giving birth, but she had started buying everything in matching sets – clothes, accessories, anything. At the salon, she would always tell the stylist to give them identical haircuts, and no one ever questioned it. Everyone seemed to believe that twins should always match. Nichika learned this every time someone gave them matching gifts.

'I'm so happy. It's like we're the same person,' Nodoka had said, smiling in the mirror at the salon.

'Yeah.'

Nichika could never say she wanted to just be herself. Their mother would be heartbroken, and Nodoka would be hurt. And so, she kept wearing the same hair, the same clothes, the same everything.

'Um, since you've got glasses on, you must be Nichika. The teacher asked me to give you this.'

But that meant most people only saw her as one half of a pair.

After entering middle school, she had started wearing fake glasses so people could tell them apart. Even so, once she took them off, distinguishing between them was like playing an impossible spot-the-difference puzzle.

Even now, she could probably count on one hand the number of people in this class who could confidently tell she was Nichika. Certainly not that nasty Lisa Okami, who always called them *the twins*, never by name.

Every time someone called them that, Nichika felt herself start to disappear. If she had been born as just herself, not as one half of a pair, would she have had a different kind of school life? Every time that hollow feeling crept in, she couldn't help but wonder.

'Next is an even number . . . Let's pick who will sit out.'

Karen Asakura was managing the game from the front of the class, while Lutsu Kanamori watched nervously beside her.

Nichika, who was in the student council with them, had seen up close how their friendship had grown. She remembered how patient Lutsu had been in teaching Karen, and how they had smiled together each time Karen solved a problem. It felt like just yesterday.

'Please point to the student you want to wait this round out,' Karen instructed.

As usual, everyone except Lisa pointed to Mishin Mizushima.

Nichika, however, pointed at Nodoka.

Please, let her live.

Now that her own death was sealed, that was all Nichika could pray for.

'Then Mizushima will be on standby,' Karen announced.

The result was obvious from the start. Nichika had only wanted to push death a little farther away from her sister.

Like before, the Alpha Girls would probably pair with the Beta Girls A group, while the student council members like her would go with those from Beta Girls B. Unless Lisa threw another tantrum, there was no reason to risk another reshuffle.

'Yayoi, over here! You're with me!' Lisa called, forcing her way once again.

'Okay!' Yayoi Yoitani replied brightly, running over to her.

With that, the death game resumed across the classroom. There was no time to hesitate.

Leading the speechless Nodoka by the hand, Nichika walked toward Lutsu and Karen, then quickly dropped to her knees in a deep bow.

'Lutsu, Karen . . . Please. Forget about me. Just let Nodoka live!' Her voice cracked as she begged, all pride gone.

She was essentially asking one of them to die in her place. Tears dripped onto the old wooden floor, sinking into the worn-out boards.

Even though she was doing it for her sister, her heart felt like it was splitting apart. Because Lutsu and Karen were the only two people in this class who saw her and her sister not as *the twins*, but as Nichika and Nodoka.

'Nichika . . . Please, stop,' Karen whispered.

'Yeah, lift your head. Besides, Nichika, you don't have to –'

Lutsu had just started to say something when –

'. . . It's okay, Nichika. Thank you,' Nodoka spoke. Her voice was calm, a stark contrast from the broken, panicked way she had sounded before.

Nichika stood up and, acting on instinct, grabbed her sister's narrow shoulders. 'Why would you say that?!' she couldn't stop herself from shouting.

Last time, she had held Mishin's hand, ready to die, just to keep her alive. Because she loved her more than she loved herself. But Nodoka didn't seem to understand any of that.

'. . . I'm sorry.'

In Nodoka's eyes – those same dark brown eyes glistening with tears – Nichika saw herself reflected perfectly.

'. . . I'm sorry, too,' Nichika murmured, realizing what she had done and letting go.

'It's okay. Really, Nichika. I don't need to survive anymore.'

'. . . Why not?'

Usually, as twins, they could read each other's minds. But this time, Nichika had no idea what Nodoka was thinking.

'Because even if I die, you'll still be here. That means I'll still exist in this world.'

'No . . . I'm not you.'

'Maybe not to you. But to me, us being together was what made me *me*.'

Nichika felt like her soul was leaving her body as she collapsed onto the floor.

Nodoka had known how she felt all along.

Thinking about it, of course she had – because they had always been of one mind.

All at once, without warning, someone grabbed Nichika's hand.

'Sorry to interrupt, but we're out of time,' said Yuki, frowning slightly – the same Yuki who always looked faintly unlucky despite being fairly pretty.

Being paired with Nodoka last time had backfired – most people probably still thought of Nichika as part of a set, and since she hadn't yet paired with Yuki, this was inevitable.

A wave of dread washed over her. She looked over her shoulder.

Karen was holding hands with Katsune Nakano from the Beta Girls B clique, and Lutsu with Leika Tomoe, also from that group.

She understood no one had the luxury to care about others now. She herself had asked Yuki before, dooming Yu without a second thought, and just moments ago had begged Karen and Lutsu to sacrifice themselves. Everyone had run out of options – there was no choice but to do whatever it took to survive.

But she still couldn't stop despair from swallowing her.

As the flower on Nodoka's chest began to scatter, Nichika yanked her hand away from Yuki's and rushed to embrace her sister.

'Nodoka . . . No, please, Nodoka, no . . .'

Her timid sister. She always hyperventilated whenever something shocking happened. She could never go anywhere without Nichika.

'Get back, Nichika. It's dangerous.'

'Then why . . .? Why push me away only now?'

'Nichika, I always wanted to be like you – smart like you, strong like you. Ever since we were born, I've wanted to be you,' Nodoka said, smiling as she stepped back.

Then, the final petal fell.

With a cruel blast, the corsage on Nodoka's chest exploded, and her upper body was torn apart.

All her life, Nichika had wanted to be the only one of her kind in the world.

And yet, in this world without Nodoka, she still wasn't that.

She was only half.

She realized she had committed an unforgivable sin the moment her sister's remains rained down around her.

Yes – Nichika herself hadn't yet paired with Nodoka.

Lutsu had been about to tell her that before Nodoka had spoken.

When Nichika had bowed and begged for Nodoka's life, she had been the only one who hadn't realized it.

And when Nodoka interrupted, Nichika understood – she had done it to sacrifice herself.

The wave of despair that hit her was so heavy she couldn't stand.

There was only one reason she hadn't noticed something so excruciatingly obvious – ever since they were born, Nodoka had been her, and she had been Nodoka.

Round 10

Standby: Mishin Mizushima

Sarasa Hoshikawa - Sayuki Sena
Urin Nekoya - Yayoi Yoitani
Lisa Okami -
Uta Marguerite Samejima
Lara Kagahi - Kiko Masugi
Karen Asakura - Katsune Nakano
Lutsu Kanamori - Leika Tomoe
Nichika Saeki - Yuki Koiwai

Disqualified:
Nodoka Saeki

Students Remaining: 15

Time Left:
21 minutes

Chapter 11: Unconscious Malice
Katsune Nakano

In the middle of the classroom, Nichika Saeki sat slumped in a pool of blood, her eyes empty and unfocused.

That was because her sister, Nodoka Saeki, had been disqualified in the previous round.

What did it feel like to watch someone identical to you get torn apart before your very eyes? Just trying to imagine it out of morbid curiosity sent a chill down Katsune's spine.

She wasn't a twin, but she *did* have an older sister.

They looked nothing alike – partly because her sister was overweight, but even putting that aside, their resemblance was non-existent. If anything, her classmate Leika Tomoe, who wasn't even family, looked more like her.

Yu Nikaido had once said, 'Leika and Katsune have totally different vibes, but somehow, they look alike,' and Yuki Koiwai had agreed, 'Yeah, I see it.'

It was true that both of them were fairly tall, about one hundred and sixty-five centimetres, and both had black, semi-long hair – though Katsune's was straight while Leika's was always softly curled.

But Katsune knew that when Yuki said their *vibes* were different, it wasn't about hair. It was about money.

To put it bluntly, Katsune's family was poor. That was why she was genuinely grateful when Leika, on a whim, handed her brand-name clothes or bags she didn't use anymore. She could sell them for a good price on Mercari, which became her main source of pocket money.

And that extra cash always went to her boyfriend.

'Sorry for always making you pay,' he would say. 'I can't get a part-time job 'cause of baseball practice.'

He was always busy with the team, so they only saw each other once a month. But those few hours together in the cheapest room of a Cinderella Castle-themed love hotel past Heian Shrine were, for Katsune, pure bliss.

Two years ago, Yu had invited her to a boys' school culture festival. The guy had been selling takoyaki. When she went to pay, he slipped her a note with his LINE ID and said, 'Message me if you want.' She had fallen for him instantly. Maybe it was because she went to an all-girls' school and was starved for male attention, but his face had been exactly her type.

'It's fine,' she would tell him. 'I work anyway, so don't worry about it.'

Indeed, she was juggling part-time jobs at both a convenience store and a karaoke joint. Ever since the day he had said, 'Let's move in together after graduation,' she had been saving every yen she could for that future. The thought of leaving her dim, sunless house behind and living with him in a stylish apartment like the main character in a TV drama made the long shifts feel like nothing at all.

'You can let go now, Nakano. The next round's about to start.'

Lutsu Kanamori's voice snapped Katsune back to herself. She hurried to release her hand.

She must have zoned out from exhaustion. It felt like hours had passed. Dazed, she glanced at the clock – the hands pointed to 9:40. Forty minutes had passed since the game began. She no longer knew whether that was long or short.

'It's been forever since we were partners,' Lutsu said, her voice carrying a trace of guilt.

'Has it?' Katsune didn't remember ever being paired with her. 'Maybe back in middle school?'

Lutsu nodded.

No wonder she didn't remember, Katsune thought.

They had gone to the same middle school. Which meant they had both known Mishin Mizushima, too.

They had even been in the same class in second year. They hadn't been in the same group, but they had gotten along fine as classmates. Lutsu had already had that model-student, class-rep atmosphere about her even then. And Mishin – she hadn't been the ghostlike girl she was now. Back then, she had been lively.

That was before the horrific bullying started.

Even now, the memory made Katsune's stomach twist. It had been nauseating just to watch.

The ringleader, one of the Alpha Girls, had actually enjoyed seeing Mishin pick through her lunch to avoid bugs and garbage. Katsune had been part of that ringleader's clique, but she hadn't joined in the bullying. She had just looked the other way. She had felt sorry for Mishin, sure, but she had been too scared to stand up for her. If it had been her being bullied like that, she wouldn't have survived.

That was why she had genuinely admired Lutsu, who had at least tried to stop it once.

'Hey . . . Do you remember what the teacher said before the game started? About *unconscious malice*?' Lutsu asked, her expression serious.

'Uh . . . Yeah.'

In truth, she didn't.

'That's what we are,' Lutsu said quietly.

'. . . What do you mean?'

Katsune had no idea what she was talking about. She had never felt *malice* toward anyone.

'Because since coming to this school, we never once paired up with Mishin.'

'That's just 'cause we already had friends,' Katsune said.

And Lutsu's student council group had always been a foursome, anyway. That wasn't malice.

'Do you really think so?' Lutsu's tone made it clear she was blaming herself. 'Were your group's friendships ever real, Nakano?'

'What are you trying to say?'

'Sometimes, having *no* malice is worse than having it,' she said. 'That's all I meant. Sorry. Forget it.'

With that, Lutsu turned and walked away, running toward Karen Asakura. Watching her go, anger flared in Katsune's chest.

You were just as guilty, she thought. *You looked away from Mishin's suffering, just like the rest of us.*

She wanted to shout it after her, but she didn't have the energy.

She hadn't slept at all the night before.

'*Sorry. I didn't think you were serious*,' her boyfriend had texted her.

She had asked him, '*You said we'd move in together after graduation – when should we look for a place?*' That was his reply.

'*Weren't* you *serious?*' she had written back.

'*Honestly, I barely remember saying that.*'

All she could do was let out a forced laugh. He had said that line early in their relationship. Back then, he had messaged her every day, taken her out every week, always paid. But six months later, he had gotten too busy with baseball, started meeting her only once a month and had stopped paying for things. She had known she had become nothing but convenience. She had known he was seeing other girls. But she had ignored it. She had believed that once they lived together, things would go back to how they were. She still believed it.

That was why she couldn't die here.

'This time, the number's odd, so no one has to sit out,' Karen Asakura announced clearly.

Perhaps she was getting used to being in charge. Or maybe she was just getting used to this ordeal. For the students who had survived this long, the abnormal had started to feel normal.

Katsune took a deep breath. The smell of death filled her lungs, something she had never known before.

By this point, her group – Beta Girls B – had already partnered with all the student council members.

Which meant the Alpha Girls couldn't partner with the council anymore, either.

'Let's pair up, Karen!' Lisa Okami said, swooping in right after she had finished issuing the instructions.

Katsune didn't remember all the pairings, but she was sure no Alpha Girl had joined hands with a council member yet.

And she and her group still hadn't paired with anyone from the Beta Girls A.

Who should she choose from that group? Who looked most likely to die first? Katsune was still thinking it through when Leika spoke up in her usual clueless tone.

'Hey, Katsune, who should I hold hands with next? I'm losing track of who I've already paired with!'

Katsune pretended not to hear her.

'Hey, Kiko, let's pair up!' she called instead, running over to Kiko Masugi from Beta Girls A.

'Sure,' Kiko answered easily.

Their hands met.

Out of the corner of her eye, she saw Yuki Koiwai take Sayuki Sena's hand, also from Beta Girls A.

The remaining two, Yayoi Yoitani and Uta Marguerite Samejima, suddenly realized something.

'Wait, we haven't paired yet!'

'Oh crap, you're right – let's go!'

They grabbed each other's hands in a rush.

Apparently, the Alpha Girls had started pairing outside their own group before finishing within it. Judging by Yayoi's tone, it wasn't even a plan – they had just done it without thinking. Katsune's group, on the other hand, had already exhausted all their internal pairs.

Which meant that after Yu Nikaido's disqualification – and now that Katsune and Yuki had each paired with A-group Beta Girls – Leika was the one left over.

'What do I do? What do I do?' Panicking, Leika clawed at her perfectly curled hair.

Up until now, someone – usually Yu – had always told her what to do. But neither Katsune nor Yuki had the bandwidth to babysit her anymore. Even if Leika somehow survived, it wouldn't help them.

Still, Katsune hadn't completely written her off. There was *one* way Leika could survive.

She could pair with Mishin.

'Finally!' Urin Nekoya shouted before Leika even realized it. 'I'm pairing with the *designated student*!' she announced to her phone camera set up at the back of the room, as if this were some touching, cinematic moment, then clasped Mishin's hand.

From behind Katsune sounded a merciless, mechanical chime. She didn't even need to look to know what it meant – Leika's corsage had begun to fall apart.

'What should I do? I have a dinner party tonight!' Leika whimpered.

Her obliviousness, Katsune thought, was almost inspiring in its purity.

Remembering what Lutsu had said earlier, Katsune was finally forced to admit it – she had never thought of Leika as a real friend. She had just been a money tree. The same went for everyone in their group except Yu Nikaido. Yu hadn't been much fun, but she had been a good person. Perhaps she had been the only one who truly believed their friendship was real.

'Help me . . .' Leika's voice called out.

Katsune knew it was meant for her, but she pretended not to hear.

Round 11

Lisa Okami - Karen Asakura
Sarasa Hoshikawa - Lutsu Kanamori
Lara Kagahi - Nichika Saeki
Yayoi Yoitani -
Uta Marguerite Samejima
Kiko Masugi - Katsune Nakano
Sayuki Sena - Yuki Koiwai
Urin Nekoya - Mishin Mizushima

Disqualified:
Leika Tomoe

Students Remaining: 14

Time Left:
18 minutes

Chapter 12: Hope
Kiko Masugi

At last, one of the Alpha Girls had joined hands with the designated student.

It shouldn't have been a touching moment – far from it – but somehow, it shook Kiko to the core.

Unconscious malice.

The words Ms Suzuta had said before the game began flashed through her mind.

Until now, Kiko had never felt guilty about not joining hands with Mishin Mizushima. She had her own people to pair up with, and if someone without friends was left out, well, that was just unavoidable.

Or was it? Was it really something that couldn't be helped? Maybe the fact that the sight of Urin Nekoya and Mishin joining hands felt like such a special moment showed just how numb she had become.

Kiko had never talked to Mishin. She had never even thought about trying to. She didn't know what kind of person Mishin really was, and had never really cared to find out. Because everyone in the class LINE group chat called her *the ghost*, Kiko had only ever seen her through that lens. And honestly, Mishin really *did* seem like a ghost. So, when her name came up in the calligraphy club, everyone called her *the ghost* there, too. There was no malice in it. No one meant to bully her. They were just repeating the nickname one of the popular girls had made up.

Still, Kiko was starting to *feel* like a monster.

Because if you looked at it from Mishin's perspective, what else *could* that be, except malice?

'Um . . . Since we have an even number this time . . .' Karen Asakura's voice trembled slightly as she continued to run the game.

Just standing there participating was suffocating enough, so being the one in charge of a game that led to death must have been draining her twice as fast.

'Karen? You're getting tired, huh? Hey, you don't have to run things anymore. Let's just have Mishin sit out again this round, okay? We're all done for anyway if she gets eliminated. Everyone's fine with that, right?' Urin chimed in, sounding almost considerate.

Everyone except Lisa Okami nodded. If the *designated student* got disqualified, no one else would survive. And with only eighteen minutes left on the clock, there was no time to argue about who should sit out instead. A vote would just turn into a fight.

'Alright, no time to waste – please form pairs, everyone!' Urin announced cheerfully as she waved at the camera, still recording the game's every turn.

Even now, she was using this nightmare to feed her craving for attention. Kiko shot her a look of pure disgust.

Come to think of it, wasn't Urin the one who had started calling Mishin *the ghost* in the first place?

Kiko searched her foggy memory while scanning the room.

Half the class was now gone, the possible pairings getting fewer and fewer.

Who could she even join hands with at this point? Who had she already paired with? Who was left?

Her mind was spinning.

Maybe . . . Maybe *she* would be next to die.

'Pull yourself together, Kiko.'

Her mother's voice cut through the sound of her classmates' ragged breathing and the furious spring storm battering her eardrums.

'You'll never make it in this world if you're that spineless. Remember, you're going to be a maiko after you graduate. You were supposed to start right after middle school, but you begged to go to high school despite having such awful grades, so I let you – and a private school, no less! I became a maiko right after middle school, a geiko at twenty and now, I run my own geisha house. I worked my tail off for that. When are you going to grow up?'

Hearing that familiar scolding – like a greatest hits reel of every lecture she had found herself on the receiving end of – made Kiko's head spin. She almost fainted.

'Kiko, we haven't paired up yet.'

Just as she was losing consciousness, Sayuki Sena, also from the calligraphy club, extended her hand.

Kiko didn't even think – she just grabbed it.

By the time she realized what was happening, everyone else had already found a partner.

She looked around again, needing to see who was left out.

The moment her eyes met the remaining student's, her exhausted heart gave a violent jolt.

'Hey, Kiko. Guess there really isn't any hope left in Gion, huh?' Yayoi Yoitani said with that sarcastic smile of hers.

She was Kiko's best friend, her comrade-in-arms.

Every time Kiko stepped into the calligraphy club room, the faint scent of ink brushed her nose. She loved that smell.

'We should probably start picking songs for this year's performance, huh?' their club president, Uta Marguerite Samejima, asked the other members.

It was spring, right after the seniors had graduated, and before any new first-years had joined.

Uta was half French, half Japanese. At first, Kiko had been intimidated by her Western looks, but once they started talking, she realized Uta spoke Kyoto dialect just like the rest of them – a totally normal high school girl. In fact, she was easily the best calligrapher in the club, and not just technically. Her writing showed how deeply she loved the art.

It was Uta's idea for the club to enter the National Calligraphy Performance Competition every year – a contest where teams wrote on huge sheets of paper to music. Making it past preliminaries was almost impossible for a small club like theirs, but simply practising and filming their submission video was fun enough to make it worthwhile.

'I wanna do Kana Nishino's "Best Friend"!' Sayuki said, raising her hand eagerly.

With her jet-black eyes and striking Kyoto beauty, she could have stepped out of a painting. Inside, however, she was the most trend-obsessed, fickle girl Kiko knew. She loved anything popular and changed boyfriends like new outfits. That contradiction always amused Kiko.

'That's just because you're obsessed with Kana Nishino. Rejected.' Yayoi shot her down instantly.

Something about Yayoi always gave off an old-school delinquent atmosphere. Maybe it was her intentionally long skirt, or her slightly retro hairstyle. But no one made fun of her for it – if anything, it was her signature style. And with her sharp, well-defined features, she could easily pull it off.

Early on, her bluntness had intimidated people, but by now, everyone relied on her honesty.

'Aw, come on! I just wanna do a Kana song!'

'Calligraphy isn't your fangirl hobby. And we did "Instruction Manual" last year, remember? Not that it's Kana's fault, but that was a total song-choice fail.'

'But I thought writing out "Instruction Manual" would be funny! We could do her two years in a row!'

'No way.'

As Sayuki and Yayoi bickered, Uta sighed and turned to Kiko. 'Any song you want to do?'

A melody that had been looping in her head for a month surfaced.

'It's kind of an old song . . . but a customer sang it at work, and it really stuck with me.'

'Whoa, *you* complimenting a customer's song? That's rare. What is it?' Yayoi leaned in, curious.

'It's by Southern All Stars. I'll play it on YouTube.' Kiko pulled her phone from her skirt pocket and played the song.

'. . . Yeah, that's good,' Uta said as soon as it ended. 'It's upbeat, but still kind of moving.'

'Totally hits you,' Yayoi agreed.

'I still think "Best Friend" fits better,' Sayuki said, pouting a little. 'But it's good. What's it called?'

'"Trail of Hope",' Kiko exhaled, relieved that they all seemed to like it.

'Hope, huh . . .?' Yayoi murmured, sounding thoughtful.

That sparked another memory for Kiko.

'Your dad named you Kiko for *hope*,' her mother had said after they crossed the Togetsukyo Bridge at Arashiyama during her thirteenth-year pilgrimage. 'He wanted you to grow up with hope.'

Her father had once been one of her mother's best clients. He was already fifty-five and her mother twenty-five when they got married. To be honest, Kiko had never really thought of him as a father. She was eight when he died from illness ten years ago, and all she had thought was, *Grandpa's gone.* He had spoiled her like a grandchild, not a daughter. He had been married before, too, with a son twenty years older than Kiko. He had abandoned that family for her mother.

So why, Kiko wondered, would a man swallowed by the night give *her* – a child born of sin – the name *Hope*?

'Play it again,' Uta said.

'Yeah.'

Kiko hit replay. As the melody filled the room, she could tell Uta was already planning out the performance in her head.

'I'm glad we decided on this year's song. It's a good one.'

That night, Yayoi hummed the tune under the weeping cherry trees in Maruyama Park.

'Right? But, you know, the idea of *hope* shows up in songs all the time. Do you think everyone really has it?'

Looking up at the trees, their blossoms already gone though it wasn't even two weeks into April, Kiko felt a pang of loneliness.

'No idea,' Yayoi answered instantly, and Kiko let out a small laugh of relief.

'I mean, just having parents in the nightlife business kind of kills all hope, doesn't it? Like, across the board.'

'For real.' Yayoi pointed up at the night sky with her fingers shaped like a gun and gave a little nod.

Yayoi's mum ran a bar on the fifth floor of a mixed-use building in Gion. In exchange for pocket money, Yayoi was made to help out there almost every night. Since she was still in high school, she would leave around ten, then wander through the grounds of Yasaka Shrine to shake off the smell of cigarettes, booze and middle-aged men clinging to her clothes. Eventually she would end up in Maruyama Park, zoning out under the weeping cherries.

Kiko had first seen her there one summer night in their first year, right after she had stormed out of the house following a brutal fight with her mother.

'What's up?' Yayoi asked when she saw Kiko's face, a mess of tears and snot.

'. . . I ran away from home.' Kiko sniffled hard, wiping her nose with her sleeve.

Yayoi burst out laughing. 'Seriously? That's hilarious.'

Just a little while earlier, Kiko had been so upset she had thought about dying. It had been the worst fight she had ever had with her mum. But as she ranted and Yayoi laughed and clapped her hands, somehow, it all started to seem like no big deal. Maybe it had even been her fault.

After that, it became their habit to meet late at night under the weeping cherries, talking nonsense until the small hours.

'How do you think hope is born?'

'At the very least, it sure as hell isn't born in Gion.'

'Yeah. No matter what you talk about here, it all reeks of money.'

'Money's just like a soap bubble anyway. I get three thousand yen every day, and somehow, it's gone by the end of it.'

'Don't call men soap bubbles. And maybe stop spending so much.'

'Okay, fine, I admit that. But money and men – they're kinda the same thing, aren't they?'

'Yeah. Pretty much.'

The money men earned in the daytime flowed into Gion at night. And by morning, the night's events burst and vanished like soap bubbles – just fleeting dreams.

'Who do you think's dumber, men or women?' Yayoi asked.

Somewhere nearby, a stray female cat in heat was yowling.

'Men, obviously,' Kiko said.

Women could be idiots, sure – but any guy willing to drop that much cash just to drink with one was clearly worse.

'Then if you could be reborn, would you rather be a man or a woman?' Yayoi asked again.

'A woman,' Kiko answered without hesitation.

'Why?'

'Because it's way easier being a woman.'

If she wanted to, a woman could get by without ever working, living off a man instead. But maybe that was just her bias – something she had picked up watching her mother all these years. She thought for a moment, then asked back, 'What about you, Yayoi?'

'Hmm . . . I dunno. Guess I won't know till I'm about to die.'

'What's that supposed to mean?'

'Well, I've only been alive seventeen years as a girl. Oh, by the way, one of my old middle school friends just tried to set me up with a guy. What do you think?'

Yayoi opened a LINE chat on her phone and showed Kiko a photo from a friend she didn't recognize.

'. . . He kinda looks like that YouTuber, you know, Seikin.'

'I thought the same thing.'

'I don't hate Seikin. Actually, I kinda like him.'

'For real? Me too. We've got similar taste.'

'So, you gonna go out with him?'

'Nah. I'm more into visual kei types.'

'Like Golden Bomber?'

'"Unmanly" is a masterpiece no matter how many years go by. Oh! I'm totally gonna suggest we use it for next year's performance.'

'Sayuki's gonna lose her mind.'

Their laughter melted into the Gion night.

Conversations at night were always hilarious, but by morning, they could never remember what had been so funny. Everything that happened in Gion's nights popped like bubbles and disappeared. But Kiko loved those pointless nights with Yayoi – so much more than any time she could have spent with some random guy a friend introduced her to.

Like the cherry blossoms that signalled the end of spring, petals began fluttering down from the corsage on Yayoi's chest.

'Hey, Kiko, did you know? They say the first cherry tree to bloom waits till the very last bud opens before it lets its petals fall. They say it's waiting for its friends. One of the customers told me that yesterday. He spent ninety-nine per cent of the time bragging about the dumbest stuff, but every now and then, old guys actually know something nice.' Yayoi spoke in that casual way of hers, as if she were still sitting under the weeping cherry tree.

For real.

That was what Kiko would have said, normally. But now, buried in tears, she couldn't get a word out.

'Kiko . . . I've been thinking about it since then. If I get reborn, I still wanna be a woman. Then we can sit around badmouthing men again.'

The moment Yayoi said that, the scroll with the word *Hope* on it peeled off the wall behind her, as if to foreshadow what was coming. It was one of the pieces Yayoi had written during practice, which Kiko had put up on her own.

They had never made it to the final competition. But that last year, when they performed 'Unmanly', they had gone all in. It was a precious memory of hers. The results hadn't mattered. Well, maybe they had – but more than that, writing together as one had meant something even bigger.

Maybe, Kiko thought, the feeling they had had back then – that had been hope itself.

'So, Kiko, you've got to be reborn as a woman, too, okay?'

As the last petal fell from Yayoi's corsage, a sudden column of flame shot up from her chest.

With a scream, Yayoi's body was engulfed in fire, turning black as it burned away – as if the Gion night that had swallowed their laughter was now consuming her whole.

Round 12

Standby: Mishin Mizushima

Lisa Okami - Yuki Koiwai
Urin Nekoya - Nichika Saeki
Sarasa Hoshikawa - Karen Asakura
Lara Kagahi - Lutsu Kanamori
Sayuki Sena - Kiko Masugi
Katsune Nakano -
Uta Marguerite Samejima

Disqualified:
Yayoi Yoitani

Students Remaining: 13

Time Left:
16 minutes

Chapter 13: True Friends
Uta Marguerite Samejima

'Yayoi . . . No, no . . . I can't. I can't do this . . .'

Beside Yayoi Yoitani's body, her skin charred black from the flames, Kiko Masugi collapsed, sobbing uncontrollably. For Uta Samejima, too, memories of the past three years with Yayoi in the calligraphy club came flooding back. For the first time in this whole game, her tears spilled for someone's death. As Uta rubbed Kiko's trembling back, even Sayuki Sena was hiccupping through her sobs.

Right in the middle of their grief, Urin Nekoya began her commentary, filming the scene of the calligraphy club girls mourning their friend.

'Wow, did you see that? We've finally got someone burned to death! What kind of trick could that be? The smell is *insane*! Anyway, there are sixteen minutes left in the game, and only thirteen people remaining! We're officially down to less than half!'

- Once the number of participants drops below half, every round must begin with the call, 'Please form pairs.' If this rule is broken, the round will be void.

'According to the rules, the call is now mandatory! Alright, let's see who's getting eliminated next! Since we've got an odd number this time, go ahead and *please form pairs*!'

Her vulgar tone made Uta's anger flare. Urin's high-strung cheerfulness, like she was guaranteed to survive, was too much to take in. Yet Uta couldn't say a word. A brutal headache pounded behind her eyes, like someone was hammering against her skull.

Please form pairs.

She had heard that phrase, or some variation of it, a thousand times in gym class, but now, it echoed in her head like a curse.

Who was left for her to pair with? Fighting the pain threatening to knock her down, Uta scanned the remaining students.

She could only tell for sure that two people hadn't paired yet – Yuki Koiwai from Beta Girls B and Mishin Mizushima.

She couldn't remember who Yuki had partnered with before, but Mishin had been with Urin two rounds ago. The moment those two joined hands, something twisted inside Uta.

If she remembered right, it had been Urin who first started calling Mishin *the ghost*.

'Here's the class LINE group! Use it however you want! Oh, but I don't have everyone's IDs, so I couldn't invite everyone, lol. Not the ghost and a few others.'

Uta remembered that first flippant message. Despite being called a *class group,* only twenty people had been invited. When she checked the members list, all the so-called Groundling girls were missing. Back then, neither Urin's nickname *the ghost* nor the missing members had struck Uta as strange. She hadn't thought of it as bullying – just a natural thing. Saying *the ghost* instead of Mizushima even felt kind of cute, like it gave her some charm.

For better or worse, the third-tier girls had an aura that set them apart from the Alpha and Beta ones. The things they talked about felt like they existed on an entirely separate wavelength. It must have been the same for them. None of those girls seemed to have boyfriends, and even their way of speaking felt fundamentally different.

But maybe, just maybe, all those tiny differences had been what their teacher, Ms Suzuta, had called *unconscious malice*. Maybe everyone's casual indifference had quietly created an invisible kind of bullying.

If someone had called her *the foreigner* behind her back, would she have found it endearing? Not a chance. She probably would have thought she was being bullied.

Especially if no one even talked to her.

Now, far too late, Uta couldn't stop the guilt welling up inside her. If she couldn't pair with Yuki, then she had no right to join hands with Mishin – the girl she herself had once called *the ghost*.

'Hey, your name's got *Marguerite* in it – are you, like, foreign or something?'

Uta remembered every classmate who had asked her that in elementary school.

She had been born to a French mother and a Japanese father. Technically, her blood was half and half, but no matter the angle, she took after her mother. Fair skin, sharply defined features, pale, blue-tinted eyes and naturally light hair.

'I'm Japanese,' she had always said.

She had been born and raised in Kyoto. To her, she wasn't just Japanese – she was Kyoto Japanese. That was why it infuriated her when tourists mistook her for one of them. She would get depressed every time she looked in the mirror.

'Yeah, right. No Japanese has blue eyes,' the boys in her class said bluntly.

'Don't say that,' the girls would tell them – but that didn't mean they ever included her.

Her heart was *so* Japanese, yet people kept treating her like a foreigner. She couldn't even count how many times she had cried to her father about it.

Uta loved Japan more than anyone. Maybe it was because she knew what other countries were like.

She spent New Year's in Japan, but every Christmas – *Noël* – her mother took her back to France. During the holiday season, Paris glittered with lights, the Champs-Élysées sparkling like a sea of jewels. The Bûche de Noël cakes they ate there – rich, dense chocolate shaped like tree logs – filled her whole mouth with happiness. Those trips to Paris were the highlight of her year.

But still, Japan was the place she wanted to live. She loved Japanese food, Japanese culture.

At the same time, she knew her mother loved her own country

just as deeply – and secretly longed to return. That was why Uta never cried to her mother about being treated like an outsider. And when her mother registered her full name – middle name and all – on her school forms, Uta didn't dare complain.

Uta had another reason for loving Japan – its writing.

Hiragana, katakana, kanji – she saw them all as beautiful forms of art. Ever since she was little, she would lose herself in writing characters whenever she had time to spare.

'Whoa! You've got amazing handwriting!'

That over-the-top compliment came from the girl who had ended up sitting next to her when she started middle school – Sayuki.

She had expected to be left out again in middle school. People would still see her as some kind of oddball. *The foreigner*.

Deep down, she had already given up on having a normal school life. But Sayuki had shown her a world – a view – that existed neither in Japan nor in Paris, a world only a true friend could share.

'Hey, Uta, let's go to karaoke.'

While everyone else treated her like she was her middle name, Marguerite, only Sayuki called her by her first name – Uta.

'Yeah.'

Sayuki would often invite her out to karaoke after school, and their go-to spot was the Super Jankara on Takoyakushi Street in Kawaramachi. Sayuki never seemed to get tired of queuing up Kana Nishino songs. She must have practised them endlessly, because her singing was so good it could have landed her on a TV talent show.

'I've been a Kana fan since elementary school,' she said.

Uta hadn't really been into Kana Nishino before, but after enough enthusiastic persuasion, she found herself becoming a fan, too – and before long, they started going to Kana's concerts together.

Just a month ago, in fact, they had taken the bullet train to Yokohama Arena together.

It was Kana Nishino's final live show before her indefinite hiatus – a ticket that felt like a once-in-a-lifetime break to land.

Unfortunately, both of them had been in the worst possible mood that day.

'Can you believe it? Both of us getting dumped the day before the concert?'

'Right? That's like, destiny or something.'

Uta had been dumped by her boyfriend of a year – 'I've met someone else,' he had said. Sayuki had been dumped by her younger boyfriend of three months, the one she had fallen for at first sight and chased so hard – 'You're too much for me,' he had told her.

On the bullet train, the two of them had barely managed to hold back tears, trying desperately to turn it into a funny story.

It had been Sayuki's fourth boyfriend, but Uta's first. Her first love, and her first heartbreak. She didn't think her pain was necessarily worse than Sayuki's, but while Sayuki cheerfully dug into her bento box, Uta couldn't even swallow a bite of her favourite tamagoyaki. Her heart felt like it was being torn apart. *If love hurts this much, I never want to fall in love again,* she thought, and she meant it.

At the concert, with so many songs about love, she couldn't stop herself from remembering her ex's smile – the one he had had when he still loved her. Kana's voice, beautiful enough to earn her the title Heisei Diva, finally broke through Uta's restraint, and the tears came flooding out.

Beside her, Sayuki was shouting her love and gratitude to Kana as if she had completely forgotten she had ever been dumped. Her energy was contagious, and as the concert went on, Uta found herself pulled into it, too.

Then, when the intro to the final song began – neither of them said a word, but their hearts became one. Without either of them saying anything, they both reached out and quietly took each other's hand.

'Best Friend' – a song they had sung together countless times.

As Kana's strong, crystalline voice filled the arena, and those lyrics, written in memory of a dear friend, soared over the crowd, Uta broke down crying. In that moment, she wasn't thinking about Kana Nishino or her ex-boyfriend.

She was thinking only of Sayuki – of the day she first told her that her handwriting was beautiful.

'. . . Wait. *I* don't have anyone to pair with.'

This time, Urin spoke not to the camera on her phone, but to the room as a whole.

Uta remembered someone else – Lisa Okami – saying almost the exact same thing during the first half of the game.

Uta didn't know who Urin had paired with before, but she was sure most of the Alpha Girls had already matched up with the student council members.

Right now, the pairs were Sarasa Hoshikawa with Nichika Saeki, Lara Kagahi with Karen Asakura and Lisa Okami with Lutsu Kanamori.

'Huh? Prez? Are you kidding me? Why the hell are you holding hands with Lisa? Have you lost your mind?'

Uta could understand why Urin lashed out at Lutsu. Lutsu had been openly targeted by Lisa all this time.

'Why? Because she's my friend,' Lisa answered before Lutsu could, gripping her hand tightly.

'What? As if. You were just treating her like your enemy a minute ago,' Urin growled, forgetting all about the livestream.

'Sometimes, people act like friends in public, but deep down, they can't stand each other,' Lisa fired back.

Uta could tell that jab was aimed squarely at Urin.

No one would ever say that to a *real* friend.

Which meant Lisa hated Urin – and had set this up so Urin would end up alone. Maybe she had been waiting for this chance all this time.

'Hey, are you seriously messing with me right now, Lisa? Do you even get the difference in our worth as human beings? You're just some random nobody. I'm an influencer with three hundred thousand subscribers. When *I* promote a product, it sells out. When *you* do it, nobody buys a thing. You have *zero* impact. When you die, maybe your parents will cry. But when *I* die, at least three hundred thousand fans will mourn me. I think it's pretty obvious which one of us deserves to live.'

'Maybe. But you're the one who's about to die,' Lisa said with a small, mocking smile.

'Yeah, right.'

'You are. Don't worry, I'll take over your stream after you're gone.'

'You couldn't handle it.'

'If *you* can do it, anyone can.'

Urin's fury finally boiled over. With a shriek like a cat ready to pounce, she kicked Lisa's desk. A magazine flew out – Nicole Fujita on the cover. Lisa's, naturally.

'. . . So, what, you planned this from the start?'

'You were waiting for me to die, too, weren't you? You were lying when you said you just grabbed someone's hand at random last time, weren't you? You were trying to kill me, using that empty little head of yours to figure out how.'

'Yep! I've always hated you, Lisa-Lisa!' Urin said it with a picture-perfect smile, the kind meant to look cute for the camera.

Uta was shocked. They had always seemed close, like true friends. She never would have guessed they hated each other this much.

'Hey, Prez,' Urin said, turning to Lutsu. 'Let go of that airheaded, self-obsessed loser and hold hands with me instead. It's not too late.'

'You're the idiot,' Lisa snapped. 'Once you've paired up, it's over. You know that.'

Out of the corner of her eye, Uta saw something that made her pause – Mishin was reaching for Katsune Nakano's hand. It was the first time since the start of the game that Uta had seen Mishin initiate a pairing herself. Katsune looked stunned. Why had Mishin chosen her?

A heartbeat later, a cold sweat broke out across Uta's skin. She didn't have time to wonder.

'Sayuki, we've got to hurry and pair up, too,' Uta said, grabbing her arm.

'Y-yeah . . . But what about Kiko?'

They both turned toward Kiko. She was still kneeling beside Yayoi's charred body, unwilling to move. Maybe she wanted to die with her. Uta understood that feeling.

'Who else can you pair with, Sayuki? I can still go with Yuki, but – '

She stopped mid-sentence as realization hit her.

There were only five of them left who hadn't paired up – Uta, Sayuki and Kiko from the calligraphy club, plus Yuki from the Beta Girls B group, and Urin, who had just said she couldn't pair with anyone.

And Sayuki had been paired with Kiko last round.

'. . . Yuki probably hasn't paired with Kiko yet,' Sayuki whispered. 'Hurry, go pair with her. I feel bad for Kiko, but . . . I want *you* to live.'

There was a tremble in her voice. She had already accepted that she was going to die this round. Maybe she had known it since the start. In truth, Uta felt the same way.

'. . . But –'

'Please, go! Before Yuki grabs Kiko's hand!'

Uta had never seen Sayuki so desperate, shouting like that.

Overwhelmed by her friend's urgency, Uta nodded and turned her back on her.

She started walking slowly toward Yuki, who stood calm and still in the corner, not rushing to grab anyone. She could still pair with either Uta or Kiko, so she wasn't in danger of being left out.

But if I take Yuki's hand . . . then Sayuki will die. And so will Kiko . . .

Uta stopped, biting her lip. Every moment of her youth flashed before her – the smell of ink in the clubroom, the laughter of her friends, the morning greetings, the photobooth sessions that went on until they looked perfect, the all-night karaoke sessions that left their voices hoarse, the school trip to Tokyo where they spent all their time talking about their boyfriends under the Skytree, the night at Yokohama Arena when they held hands listening to 'Best Friend'.

Sayuki was in every single memory.

Uta turned around and ran back to her.

Then, once again, she took Sayuki's hand.

'. . . Sorry. I just wanted to hold it one more time,' Uta beamed, squeezing her hand tightly – an act that all but said she had chosen to die with her.

'Why . . .?' Sayuki whispered, tears spilling from her beautiful dark eyes.

'. . . Because we're best friends, right?' Uta smiled.

She didn't know how much she really meant to Sayuki – but to Uta, Sayuki had been her very first friend.

Her first *true* friend.

Round 13

Lisa Okami - Lutsu Kanamori
Sarasa Hoshikawa - Nichika Saeki
Lara Kagahi - Karen Asakura
Kiko Masugi - Yuki Koiwai
Katsune Nakano - Mishin Mizushima

Disqualified:
Sayuki Sena
Uta Marguerite Samejima
Urin Nekoya

Students Remaining: 10

Time Left:
14 minutes

Chapter 14: Alpha Girls
Sarasa Hoshikawa

Sayuki Sena and Uta Marguerite Samejima collapsed still holding hands, passing away as if they had simply fallen asleep.

It might have been the most beautiful – if *beautiful* was the right word – way anyone had died so far.

In the Groundling's resident-weirdo group, Setsuna Kuroki and Natsuki Himuro had touched fingertips in some kind of mysterious ritual reminiscent of the *E.T.* movie poster just before they were disqualified, but they hadn't died as a pair. In other words, the first ones to actually get disqualified for properly holding hands again were Uta and Sayuki.

Urin Nekoya had been helplessly disqualified after that, and now she was in a horrific state. Some kind of caustic chemical leaking from her corsage had melted deep into the left side of her chest, exposing part of her organs. Her uniform had ripped across the top, leaving her remaining right breast spilling out. Sarasa couldn't help remembering that time Urin pretended to do a striptease.

'Hey viewers, check it out – this is influencer Urin's gorgeous boob!' Lisa Okami filmed Urin's grotesque chest, cackling like she was having the time of her life.

'Hey, Lisa . . . Did you seriously set things up so Urin would get disqualified just now . . .?' Sarasa approached her carefully, scared of the answer.

'Yeah, so? I mean, she did it first, so I just paid her back,' Lisa said with a half-smile, then aimed the phone's camera at Sarasa.

'You two weren't friends?' Sarasa asked again, avoiding the lens.

Unable to hold back, Lisa burst into a fit of explosive laughter. 'Come on, Sarasa, never mind that . . . Didn't you know? Urin always made fun of you, calling you a lesbian behind your back.'

'Huh . . .?'

'She said you were still a virgin because you were *seriously* into Lara. She laughed about it all the time.'

The next second, Sarasa wet herself. She had been holding it in so long, and now, the shock and humiliation knocked her senseless.

'Wait, no way. Sarasa, did you pee yourself?' Lisa said in a syrupy voice, like she was talking to a toddler.

Without holding back, she pointed the camera in her direction. Needless to say, the phone with the bunny-ear case she was waving around belonged to Urin.

'Use this, Sarasa.' Lara Kagahi held out an orange towel, snapping Sarasa back to herself.

'I – I . . . I'm sorry.'

Her face burned crimson. It was the towel Lara always used at practice, and Sarasa hesitated to take it, but looking at her soaked lower body, she didn't have the luxury of pride.

'I can't take this anymore. I wish I was dead.'

She didn't actually mean she wanted to die. She wanted to say she was embarrassed to death. But as soon as she said it, she regretted using those words at a time like this.

'We can't leave the classroom, so it can't be helped. Honestly, I kinda wanna go too. Maybe I should.'

Lara's breezy tone was her own way of softening the blow, making sure she didn't hurt Sarasa. That kind gesture squeezed Sarasa's heart tight.

'Hey, Sarasa, you okay?' Still filming with a nasty grin, Lisa tilted her head in fake concern.

Lara silently walked up to her, then snatched the phone out of Lisa's hand and hurled it hard into the hallway, like she was passing a basketball mid-game.

'You're disgusting,' Lara glared, her long, sharp eyes colder than ever.

Sarasa couldn't help staring. More than anything, she was touched that Lara had gotten angry on her behalf.

'Well, enjoy playing hero while you can, Prince,' Lisa purred, pressing a finger with vivid pink nails against Lara's lips.

'What now?' Lara brushed her hand away like shooing a mosquito.

'Hmm. I just wonder if our dear prince realizes she's getting disqualified this round?' Lisa said in a voice so sweet it was nauseating.

'. . . Looks like I am,' Lara muttered after glancing around at the remaining students.

Sarasa knew it, too. She remembered everything about Lara better than she remembered herself.

'Lara . . . How can you act so calm?' Sarasa's voice trembled.

The urine soaking her socks had gone cold and clammy.

'. . . Everyone dies someday.'

Sarasa couldn't tell if that was bravado or how she truly felt. She never understood what Lara was thinking. She only knew she couldn't bear the thought of her dying.

'. . . I don't want that. I can't handle losing you! Because . . . Because I . . .'

I –

She clamped her mouth shut before she finished.

Sarasa remembered the entrance ceremony three years ago like it was yesterday.

She had been standing under a cherry tree, staring up at its foliage in full bloom. She didn't normally care about flowers, but today, something about cherry blossoms, about new beginnings, seemed to have a magnetic pull.

What was that?

Catching a glimpse of something sparkling among the petals, she stretched up on her toes to reach for it. But it was just light. Sunlight glinting off the blossoms, tricking her eyes into seeing something mesmerizing.

'Ugh, great.'

As she turned to leave, she realized her hair was caught on a branch.

The ceremony was about to start. She sighed, helpless.

That was when a sleepy-looking prince appeared in front of her. This was an all-girls school, but she looked like she had walked right out of a teenage romance manga.

'What are you doing?' the prince asked, staring at Sarasa like she was some kind of curiosity.

'M-my hair got stuck . . . I can't move,' she explained, flustered.

The prince stepped close and deftly untangled her hair from the branch. Then, she slipped off a simple black hair tie from her own wrist and gathered Sarasa's dishevelled hair into a neat ponytail.

'This way, it won't get caught again,' she said with a smile.

Sarasa's heart leapt so hard it felt like she had been launched out of her own body, like a goldfish flopping out of its tank, gasping for air. Even after the prince said, 'See you', and walked off, Sarasa's heart kept thrashing. She didn't need anyone to tell her – that pain was the beginning of love.

Lara had been so tall that Sarasa assumed she was in a higher class, but during the ceremony, she learned they were both new students.

'I'm Lara Kagahi. I like sleeping. My special skill is basketball.'

That was how Sarasa learned the prince's name during homeroom.

It didn't take long to become friends. She prided herself on how easily she made them – acting familiar had never made anyone dislike her. She had never had reason to fear being disliked.

But no matter how close she got, it never felt like she would get beyond *friend*. She didn't know what to do. She had only ever dated boys, and the idea of asking Lara how she felt – whether she even liked girls – terrified her.

Time drifted on. With nowhere to put her feelings, Sarasa spent three whole years tying her hair with the elastic Lara had given her. Every time she did so, she remembered that moment. She never forgot the feeling of Lara's hands in her hair.

And just like Urin had said behind her back, Sarasa was a virgin. She had avoided that sort of thing back in middle school.

But wanting to touch Lara was another story entirely – and wanting Lara to touch her. Countless times. She had always felt it. Whenever they were paired up, she felt that warmth.

'Since it's even-numbered this time, we'll have to pick someone to sit out! Who votes for Mizushima?' Stomping over Urin's corpse, Lisa took charge without bothering to ask for anyone's agreement.

As someone from the same Alpha Girls clique, Sarasa had sensed Lisa's bitter envy long ago. Ever since Urin became a popular YouTuber, something in their relationship had shifted.

This time, only three out of ten students voted for Mishin Mizushima.

Only Lutsu, Nichika and Karen from the student council raised their hands. It was the obvious result. Sitting out this round or pairing with Mishin would delay disqualification one more time. That went for Lara, too, which was why Sarasa didn't raise her hand, either.

'Please, everyone! Let Lara sit out this time!' Sarasa begged the surviving students, clasping her hands in prayer.

All she wanted to do was save Lara. There was no malice involved, and she wasn't thinking of rank or privilege. Speaking her feelings felt perfectly natural. But that was exactly the arrogance born from one who had always been favoured.

Normally, someone else would have spoken up to agree with her, saying, 'Okay, let's do that.'

But now, no one answered. Everyone stared at the floor.

The eager classmates who used to respond to her instantly now felt like a mirage.

Cold logic said this reaction made sense. Helping Lara benefited none of them. With the end of the game in sight, everyone wanted to survive.

Sarasa turned to her final hope – Mishin – and bowed deeply. 'Please, Mizushima, vote for Lara. Even if you don't sit out, you have lots of choices to pair up with. Please.'

Mishin held Sarasa's gaze, a sad expression falling across her face. Sarasa couldn't read what it was meant to convey.

'. . . I can't vote for Lara,' Mishin answered after a pause.

'Why not?'

'Because . . . there's someone else I want to vote for.'

That was unexpected.

'. . . Who?'

Mishin pointed.

Lutsu Kanamori . . .? No – the girl standing behind her, Karen Asakura.

Sarasa could pull up the memory of the day Karen transferred into their class as vividly as if it had just happened.

The moment Karen walked into the classroom, something deep inside Sarasa flared with violent jealousy. Not because Karen looked better than her – though she did – but because someone that stunning looked like she belonged standing beside Lara. She couldn't help imagining the nightmare scenario – if Karen ever made a move on her, what would Lara do?

'Wow, so you're Sarasa Hoshikawa. Even your name's cute.'

Their desks ended up next to each other, and when Karen praised her like that, even Sarasa's heart skipped a beat. Karen had that kind of impossible glow.

And Karen's beauty wasn't only skin-deep. In gym class, she had volunteered to pair with Mishin, who by then had long been the class ghost. Sarasa had never considered pairing with Mishin. She had never thought to talk to her. It wasn't malicious – it just felt natural not to bother with someone she didn't need to talk to.

But was that really natural? Was it truly free of malice?

'. . . I've never talked to Hoshikawa or Kagahi, so I can't vote for either of you,' Mishin continued as if she could see straight through her.

Now, as she looked at Sarasa, there was something unmistakably contemptuous in her eyes.

Sarasa couldn't say a word. Lara remained silent, too.

'So, who're *you* voting for? We're out of time here,' Lisa demanded, turning to the students who hadn't raised their hands yet.

Perhaps influenced by Mishin, the surviving Beta Girls – Kiko Masugi, Katsune Nakano and Yuki Koiwai – pointed at Karen.

That made it four votes for Karen and three for Mishin. If Sarasa and Lara voted for Karen, Karen would have to sit this round out. And Lara might live.

Just as hope flickered to life, Lara pointed at Mishin. She was accepting her own disqualification.

'Vote, Sarasa,' Lara said. Her tone implied she meant *for Mishin*.

Sarasa shook her head and pointed at Karen instead.

Four to five.

'Huh. We can't start the game like this, so fine, *I'll* vote for Karen, too,' Lisa muttered, annoyed. It was obvious she thought *she* was the one who deserved to sit out.

Had Sarasa's face looked that arrogant when she had begged for Lara earlier? Was this the selfishness Ms Suzuta had called *unconscious malice*? Of course it was. Mishin's sad expression finally made sense – Sarasa hadn't realized her own ugly streak at all. Now, having been made aware of it, she wished she could vanish.

'Alright then, *please form pairs*!' Lisa's voice, utterly devoid of tension, couldn't have been more out of place given the situation,

Lined up and ready, Lutsu moved first, grabbing Mishin's hand. She liked playing the good girl, but she was just as desperate to survive as anyone else. And of course, no one wanted to die.

Now that it had been decided, Sarasa no longer felt despair over Lara's fate.

'. . . Hey, Lara. Can I hold your hand again?' She looked up at Lara, who was watching the game with her usual cool, unreadable face.

Sarasa still hadn't taken Katsune's hand. She could still survive this round.

But a world without Lara meant nothing to her.

'Why?'

Just like that day, Lara stared at her like she was trying to figure out some strange creature.

'. . . Because I love you so much, it could kill me.'

Yes, kill her. And this time, saying it wasn't wrong.

'. . . Ah. I see.' Lara nodded twice, then smiled faintly at Sarasa's tearful face.

Sarasa still didn't understand her. Three years of watching her, and she might not know a thing. But knowing nothing – or knowing everything – wouldn't change this feeling.

'Lara, can you do me one last favour?'

There was one sensation she still needed to know.

'What?'

'I want to kiss you.' She tried to say it lightly, jokingly even, but tears spilled out anyway.

Lara leaned in and kissed her, wiping the tears trailing from her cheeks onto her lips.

In that moment, Sarasa felt like she could die without regret.

She squeezed the hand she had ached to hold for so long, letting herself sink into the sensation she had spent years longing to make come true.

Round 14

Standby: Karen Asakura

Mishin Mizushima - Lutsu Kanamori
Lisa Okami - Nichika Saeki

Disqualified:
Sarasa Hoshikawa
Lara Kagahi
Kiko Masugi
Katsune Nakano
Yuki Koiwai

Students Remaining: 5

Time Left:
10 minutes

Chapter 15: I Wish for Your Death
Karen Asakura

I wish for your death.

Ever since this special lesson got underway, or maybe since the day Mishin Mizushima told her that flower's meaning, those words had been stuck in Karen's chest like barbs.

Bodies of disqualified students were strewn everywhere, the classroom turned into something straight out of hell. Karen walked slowly toward the side of the room, careful not to step on any corpses. Through a window someone had opened to let the stench out, she could see the flowerbeds outside – snowdrops being pummelled by huge, bullet-like raindrops.

Last round, five students had been disqualified all at once. Sarasa Hoshikawa and Lara Kagahi, who had held hands again, had died as peacefully as Uta Marguerite Samejima and Sayuki Sena had. Maybe this special lesson was testing bonds somehow, like a friendship game. There was a clear difference in cruelty between being the odd one out and losing versus losing because you paired up with the same person again. But no matter the reason, the result was always the same – disqualification meant death.

Remembering how Katsune Nakano died made Karen want to vomit. After Sarasa chose to die with Lara, Katsune was disqualified next. Horrible insects unlike anything she had seen before crawled out of her corsage, forcing their way into her mouth. She had died thrashing in agony.

As for the other two . . . Kiko Masugi, the last survivor of the calligraphy club, died burned pitch-black beside her best friend Yayoi Yoitani, just as she had. And the moment Lutsu Kanamori grabbed Mishin's hand, Yuki Koiwai, left without a partner, collapsed and suffocated as the petals scattered from her corsage.

Compared to those two more orthodox deaths – if you could

even call them that – Katsune's felt like it was meant as a specific punishment. There had to be a reason each person died differently.

. . . If she were disqualified, what kind of torment would *she* have to endure?

The thought made Karen suddenly terrified of death.

'Hey, since this is finally the last one, Prez, can you run it?' Lisa Okami asked, as spitefully infuriating as always.

Mishin, Karen, Lisa, Lutsu and Nichika Saeki.

Only five of them were left.

'Well, *you're* not the one who's gonna survive, Karen. I am.'

Lisa positioned herself at Mishin's side, obviously meaning to grab her hand the moment the round began. Karen swallowed hard. It wasn't that she thought she deserved to survive, but she could say with certainty that it was wrong to let Lisa partner with Mishin at the very end.

Karen was sure of it – that wasn't the conclusion this special lesson was supposed to arrive at.

She looked at Lutsu, who stared back, her face equally grim. She must have realized the same thing.

But there was no more time to hesitate.

Only nine minutes remained.

'Alright . . . Please form pairs,' Lutsu said, her voice positively radiating resolve.

Just as expected, Lisa grabbed Mishin's hand, immediately forming a pair.

'I win! Ha-ha-ha!' Shrieking with manic joy, Lisa continued to clutch Mishin's hand as she tore around the classroom.

Ah. This really is the end.

Karen lowered her head, steadying her breath and letting the sound of the rain drown out the shrill, ugly cries.

'Hey, hey, how's it feel knowing you're about to get disqualified? Such a shame – you were born so cute and all.'

Lisa leaned in close, taunting her.

Karen shook off the malice and turned around. Nichika was gathering up what was left of Nodoka's dismembered upper body.

Nichika had already paired up with everyone left in the room. That meant this round, she was automatically out.

'Nichika . . . I'm sorry,' Lutsu said, approaching her. 'It's my fault. I should have said something when I had the chance.'

'No. It's not your fault. And it's not Karen's, either. The truth is, I didn't forget that I wasn't holding Nodoka's hand. It's just . . . it wasn't something you could forget or remember. Like Nodoka said – because she was me. And I was her.' Nichika stood up. Her eyes, the same deep brown as Nodoka's, flicked between Karen and Lutsu. 'Thank you for being my friends all this time. I really loved you both. You two were the only ones in this class who saw me as myself, not as one of *the twins*. I know you might not like hearing me say this, but I always hated being a twin. I hated knowing I wasn't the only me in the world. But when Nodoka died, when I became half of what I was, I realized she and I had always been one.' Against the pounding rain, Nichika's smile shone almost painfully bright. 'So please, don't worry about me anymore. Hurry. Hold hands, you two.'

Then, as if to close the curtain on everything, she said –

'Huh . . .?'

'What the hell are you talking about, Twin?' Lisa's voice broke through, dull and confused. 'Those two are best friends. They've already been holding hands.'

Nichika's expression twisted, that radiant smile gone, her face now contorted with demonic fury. 'They *haven't*. And by the way, you always call me *Twin*, don't you? You know what? *You're* the one person I hoped wouldn't make it out of this. That's why I'm so happy you're getting disqualified.'

Her voice carried a venom Karen had never heard from her before.

'Listen, I couldn't care less what someone like you thinks of me, but don't start spouting crap about me being disqualified. My victory's already decided.'

'You really don't get it? If I were lying, our flowers would already be wilting.'

In every round so far, as soon as the last pair joined hands and the disqualified was decided, the petals on that person's corsage would start to fall.

This time, however, more than thirty seconds had passed since Lisa and Mishin had paired up – and nothing had happened.

'Go on, Karen. Take Lutsu's hand.'

With Lisa paling fast as the realization hit her, Karen took Lutsu's hand just as Nichika urged her to.

Back in the first round, when everyone had paired off with their best friends, those two hadn't.

Karen had gone with Nichika. Lutsu had gone with Nodoka.

That was because Lutsu had quietly hinted, 'If you pair up now, neither of you will survive.'

The idea of not pairing with Lutsu hadn't even crossed Karen's mind – but Lutsu, foresighted as she was, must have already anticipated this moment.

'Hey, hey, how's it feel knowing you're about to get disqualified?'

Nichika leaned into Lisa's face, throwing her taunt back at her as the petals on her chest began to scatter.

'Nooo! Shut up, shut the hell up! No one else has the right to live but *meee*!' her frenzied scream filled the classroom.

Right – because by holding hands with Mishin this round, Lisa had no one left to pair with next time.

Meaning, she was finished.

But then, without warning, Lisa started laughing, like a switch had been flipped.

'A-ha-ha! I'm such a genius! I'll just pair up with Ghostie again! Then *everyone* dies!'

Cunning in the worst possible way, Lisa kept on laughing. And sure enough, if she and Mishin paired again in the next round, then Karen and Lutsu – already paired now – couldn't do so again, meaning *everyone* would be disqualified.

But the one she had called *Ghostie*, Mishin, looked on the verge of tears. She couldn't have known that was what they called her behind her back.

At that moment, Karen felt two things rise inside her – the urge to kill Lisa, and guilt for not stopping that cruel nickname.

Nichika must have felt the same.

Before anyone could react, her hand shot out and ripped the corsage from Lisa's uniform.

Lisa's laughing face twisted with horror.

'If you're going to be disqualified anyway, best to get it over with early,' Nichika said, her voice carrying a sarcastic bounce.

- Anyone who removes their corsage will be disqualified. Anyone whose corsage is removed by another student will also be disqualified.

According to the rules written on the blackboard, Nichika – already marked for disqualification – wasn't breaking any rule by removing Lisa's corsage before her own inevitable death.

In fact, it was the surest way to take Lisa down with her.

'You little bitch! I'll kill you!'

'It's fine. I'm dying anyway.'

Nichika smiled – and in that instant, her corsage detonated. Her upper body was blown apart. Blood and flesh rained down, splattering over the pile of Nodoka's remains she had gathered earlier.

Karen couldn't tell which pieces belonged to which twin anymore.

A moment later, the flowers ripped from Lisa's ample chest began to wilt.

'Aaahhh! You bastards! Die! All of you *diiieee*!'

Lisa lunged toward Lutsu. Even without announcing her intention, it was obvious – she was going to tear off Lutsu's corsage like Nichika had done to her.

But Lutsu didn't need to run.

'Ah . . .'

Lisa hadn't made it three steps before she tripped, gracelessly, over the mangled arm of Urin's corpse.

As she hit the floor, her corsage petals scattered all at once. Her body convulsed violently, almost as if she were climaxing.

'Ah, ah, ah, ah . . .'

Her groans filled the room.

Then, moving with cursed, unnatural jerks, she began strangling herself – her fingers, nails painted vivid pink, always busy scrolling on her phone, were now digging into her own throat. She kept squeezing until she stopped breathing.

It was, in a way, the perfect death for her – as if it had been scripted from the start.

Karen. Lutsu. Mishin.

With twenty-four bodies around them, they were the only three still breathing.

Suddenly, as if nothing at all had happened, silence filled the classroom.

'. . . Nichika saved us,' Karen murmured, her small voice like a drop of water breaking the stillness.

She had worked with Nichika on student council activities, had been closer to her than to most of their classmates. She had liked her. But no tears came to her eyes. Not because she had grown numb to death, but for something deeper, something broken inside her.

'Yeah. She really did. At least now, I don't have to die holding Lisa's hand,' Lutsu said.

'. . . What do you mean?

Karen knew the question was cruel.

Even she had realized it by now, so there was no way Lutsu hadn't – she could no longer pair with anyone.

'Karen . . . From the very beginning of this game, I've wanted you two to survive. That's all I've wanted. It's why I've fought so hard to stay alive.' Her eyes were steady as she addressed them both. There could be no doubt she meant every word. 'So, Karen, hold hands with Mishin.'

Now, the only new pair that could form was Karen and Mishin.

But Karen couldn't bring herself to nod along in agreement.

'I can't be the one to live, Lutsu. I don't deserve it . . .'

Even though she had made it this far, she had been carrying that feeling since the game began.

Maybe ever since before she transferred to this school – since *that* incident.

'That's not true. You're the only one who paired with Mishin in this class. You're the only one of us who deserves to live.'

'No, Lutsu. You're wrong. I just . . . wanted to atone.'

'Atone? For what?'

'. . . Before I transferred here, I stopped going to school for a while.'

Mishin stared silently at her. She already knew this – Karen had told her once. But clearly, she hadn't told Lutsu.

'Karen . . .? Why?'

Lutsu's expression was one of disbelief, just as Mishin's had been when she first heard it.

Karen turned away from them both, exhaled slowly, and said, '. . . Because I killed someone.'

In that instant, the furious sound of the rain outside cut off mid-roar.

'Karen the Karen!' someone called out, stopping her just as she was about to leave the classroom.

That was what her friends in Tokyo used to call her sometimes.

It wasn't bullying. If anything, she had been one of the popular ones – the centre of her class's social circle. *Karen the Karen* was just a dumb nickname, based on nothing more than the stigma an internet meme had attached to her name.

'We're going to Shibuya now. You're coming, right?'

'Oh, yeah, sure.'

'Then let's go! Oh, and guess what – some scout stopped me in Harajuku yesterday! I might actually get signed!'

'No way! That's so you, Lisa. I got scouted too the other day – but it turned out to be for porn.'

'Lol! Well, Tsubasa, you do kind of have that vibe.'

By some stupid coincidence, the leader of their trio had also been named *Lisa*. It was always the three of them – Lisa, Tsubasa and Karen.

Karen knew she was only in that group because of how she looked. She wasn't smart, she wasn't athletic, she couldn't sing and she didn't have any special talent or taste. Her looks were just something she was born with, not something she could take pride in.

In that group, looks were everything. Both Lisa and Tsubasa were the kind of girls who got stopped by talent scouts just for walking down the street. They posted constantly on social media, soaking in endless 'Cute!' comments from their followers – but the words meant nothing to them anymore.

'I met this hot guy on Instagram, from that elite private school in Setagaya. We're hanging out next week,' Lisa said at the Shibuya Starbucks overlooking the scramble, showing off his profile.

'Wow, he actually *is* hot. Lucky.'

'Didn't you just get a boyfriend, Tsubasa?'

'Yeah, but I don't really like him. We hooked up once and it just kind of happened.'

'Ugh, same . . . So, Karen, when are you finally getting a smartphone? You should totally do Instagram. You'd blow up on it.'

'No kidding. Who even uses flip phones anymore? What is this, the Stone Age?'

'Uh, Tsubasa? There weren't flip phones in the Stone Age. But seriously, get one already – it'd be so much easier to text you. And what'll you do when you get a boyfriend?'

'Yeah, I know . . . But I'm not really into social media, and I don't need a boyfriend right now.'

'What do you mean, *not right now*? We're in our prime, girl!'

'. . . You're so weird, Karen,' Tsubasa said.

'Yeah,' Lisa added, laughing. 'If you weren't cute, you'd totally get bullied.'

'No kidding.'

They laughed. Karen laughed, too.

Every day she laughed that same laugh, sandwiched between their shallow jokes. It was easier that way. It was normal. Karen didn't have a sense of her own self, just a routine she drifted through.

That was why she had been drawn to Kana Sasahara.

During gym, when the teacher said, 'Pair up,' Karen always ended up with Kana. Lisa and Tsubasa always partnered with each other, and Kana, who didn't belong to any other group, would be left over. There was an even number of students in their class, so no one ever had to partner with the teacher.

Kana was in the art club. After school, Karen often passed the art room and saw her painting vivid, colourful flowers. She wondered how the world looked through eyes that saw beauty like that. Every time she watched Kana's brush move, she wanted more and more to talk to her.

'That's a beautiful painting. Do you like flowers, Sasahara?'

It had been a cold winter afternoon, near the end of their first year, after class duty. Kana was alone in the art room, and Karen couldn't stop herself from calling out to her.

'Yeah.' Kana looked surprised at first, then nodded.

Even though they had been paired up in gym a few times, Karen knew she probably didn't think highly of her.

After all, Kana's isolation was the ripple effect of Lisa's contempt. That summer, Lisa had started ignoring her – for something as stupid as 'It pisses me off when that bottom-of-the-heap nobody talks to me like an equal.' The rest of the class followed suit.

So, of course, Kana probably thought Karen was the same kind of person.

'Why do you like flowers?' Karen asked anyway.

'Because they're beautiful,' Kana said. 'And they don't hurt anyone.'

Karen's chest tightened. She knew then that Kana was hurting.

'I'm . . . sorry,' Karen forced out.

'Why are you apologizing?'

Kana's voice was calm – no fear, no deference, none of the fawning tone people used with the top-tier girls like her.

'I don't know . . . I just feel like I should,' Karen said truthfully, even though she wasn't sure *why* it felt true.

Kana's lips softened into a small smile.

It was the first time Karen had seen her smile. She felt a rush of emotion. It was like watching a bud finally bloom.

'. . . You're kind of funny, Asakura,' Kana said at last.

'Am I?'

Karen couldn't grasp why Kana would think that.

'Yeah. Funny,' Kana said again, smiling.

They kept talking, cautiously learning about each other, until, before they knew it, the dismissal chime rang through the school grounds.

'Hey, is it okay if I come talk to you again sometime?' Karen asked.

'You don't need my permission to talk to me. Or to ignore me,' Kana said as she cleaned up her paints. She was right, of course.

After that day, Karen started dropping by the art room about once every two weeks – always on Thursdays, when club activities were off and Kana would come in to paint on her own.

'So, you want to be a painter, Kana?'

'Yeah. My dream is to hold a solo exhibition one day, with flowers as the main theme.'

'That's a beautiful dream.'

Karen found herself dazzled by her clarity. Kana was working toward something real, while she herself couldn't even decide on a future path.

'When it happens . . . will you come see it, Karen?'

'Of course! I'll be there, no matter what! We're best friends, after all,' Karen said, standing up and taking Kana's hand without thinking.

She was so happy hearing Kana call her by her first name. It felt different from when Lisa and the others said it – this time, her name actually *meant* something. And she knew that what she felt wasn't just friendship – it was something only best friends could feel.

'Thanks.'

Kana squeezed her hand back. It was warm, and streaked with bright, colourful paint.

'Hey, Karen the Karen. Are you like, *friends* with Kana Sasahara? Tsubasa said she saw you two together in the art room yesterday,' Lisa asked about six months after Karen started talking with Kana – right before summer break.

'Oh, um . . . I just thought her paintings were pretty, so I wanted to say something,' Karen answered timidly.

'You two text or anything?'

Karen shook her head. It wasn't a lie. She still had a flip phone, and besides, she had never seen the point of talking through social media anyway.

'Huh. You know, Karen, I get that you've got, like, low self-esteem and all, but it's kinda impressive you can talk so casually with someone from the bottom-tier crowd. Still, hanging around with her makes us look bad, so maybe stop, okay?'

Makes us look bad?

Being with you *drags* me *down a lot more, Lisa.*

Karen almost spoke her thoughts out loud, but she stopped herself.

'Yeah . . . you're right,' she said instead, forcing a weak smile.

When summer break ended, Karen and Kana went back to being nothing more than partners for gym class.

Unless Karen went to the art room after school, they didn't talk at all. Sometimes, Kana looked like she wanted to say something. During gym, when they were paired up again, she looked like she was about to speak. And of course, Karen wanted to talk, too – she had been thinking about Kana all summer. But she ignored her. Somewhere deep down, she was scared of angering Lisa.

She told herself she would go visit the art room again once things had cooled down.

But she never got the chance.

Because Kana jumped from the school roof.

Karen hadn't known.

She hadn't known Kana was being bullied.

It wasn't the kind of bullying you could see.

'Hey, what gives an ugly loser like you the right to act all high and mighty?' 'Aren't you embarrassed painting those kindergarten-level flower pictures?' 'You look so happy when Karen compliments you, but she's just being nice, you know?' 'One of the art club seniors said you've got the least talent.' 'Come on, hurry up and realize your life's worthless already.'

It had all started the day Lisa said, 'Hanging around with her makes us look bad.'

Since Karen didn't have a smartphone, she only found out later – on the news, of all places – that the class's LINE group had been that kind of hell. Kana's parents had sent the screenshots to a TV station.

Kana's death became national news for a while. Her classmates all said things like, 'It wasn't even that bad.' Not one of them looked remorseful. If anything, they seemed resentful – like they couldn't understand why they were being cast as murderers.

'It wasn't *that bad*?!'

Karen couldn't take it anymore. She screamed at her classmates, then stormed out of the classroom.

Her feet carried her to the art room.

In her mind's eye, she saw the same scene as the day she and Kana first talked. Yet now, most of Kana's paintings had been painted over in black. Karen understood that the paint-over wasn't the bullies' work – no doubt it was Kana's, in response to their harassment.

The messages that had filled her chat weren't just urging her to die – they were cruel enough to tear apart any hope she had left to live or to paint again.

But there was one painting left untouched. It was the one Karen had first called beautiful – a painting of a white flower. When she picked it up, she saw a message written in pencil on the back.

> To Karen,
>
> Thank you for complimenting my painting.
>
> Thank you for calling me your best friend.
>
> I thought of you as my best friend too.
>
> I wish we could have talked one more time.

Clutching the painting to her chest, Karen couldn't stop the endless flow of tears streaming down her face.

If I'd only told Lisa she was wrong, that Kana was amazing. If I'd only gone to the art room to see her again. If I hadn't ignored her. If I'd just listened. Then Kana wouldn't have died.

I called her my best friend, and yet I was the one who killed her.

After that day, Karen stopped going to school.

She stayed holed up in her dim bedroom, unable to stop thinking about Kana. She could barely rest. Awake or asleep, she felt crushed beneath grief and guilt.

'You and I are going to move to Kyoto, Karen,' her mother told her around two months after Kana's death, when autumn came around.

'You know the house along the Shirakawa River in Higashiyama, where Grandma used to live? It's been cleaned up top to bottom these past two months, so for now, we'll live there together. I've already taken care of your transfer to a Kyoto high school, so don't worry. It's not quite as competitive as your old one, but it's small and it's still an all-girls school. I think you'll be able to go there without any pressure,' she explained quickly, looking pleadingly into Karen's vacant eyes.

She must have used connections to arrange the transfer. After all, Karen hadn't taken a single exam. But that was nothing new – her parents had always decided everything about her future. She never had to worry about her grades. In fact, she couldn't remember ever being pressured to study. If anything, it felt as though her parents preferred her to remain forever clueless.

Her mother was so overprotective that, even at eighteen, she still wouldn't let Karen have a smartphone.

Part of it was because Karen had been born beautiful. Her mother was always praying she wouldn't get fall prey to something like kidnapping or sexual assault. So maybe, in her own fashion, this was her way of keeping her safe. Ever since Karen was little, her mother had told her again and again about terrifying crimes that started through social media. Maybe that was why Karen had never felt any interest in it – she had been brainwashed, in a sense.

'In Kyoto, we won't know anyone. And you know . . . I'm tired of Tokyo. We'll move back when you start university, and the whole family can live together again. Your father's promised to buy a new house somewhere else. By then, everything will have blown over. So, don't worry about anything, okay? I know you didn't do anything wrong. I'm always here for you, Karen.'

Her mother stroked her head gently – but the exhaustion in her face made the reason obvious.

Kana's parents had been calling every day, wanting to vent their fury at the girl who had driven their daughter to such a miserable death. Since everyone involved was underage, names were hidden – but Karen's name had been mentioned in the chat. And in the letter Kana had left for her parents, she had written Lisa's and Tsubasa's names explicitly.

Rumours spread through the neighbourhood almost instantly, and because Karen had been in the same group as the other two, people began to suspect she had been one of the ringleaders. While Karen was locked away in her room, her mother had probably endured cruel, hateful remarks from a great many people.

But once they left town, all of it – good or bad – seemed to vanish, as if the whole incident had never happened.

Her mother gradually regained her strength, and by coming to a place as unfamiliar as Kyoto, Karen felt like she too could start afresh. The guilt and sorrow would never disappear, not in this lifetime – but she wanted, even if just a little, to be free from that incident. Otherwise, she felt she might die herself.

'I'm Karen Asakura. Nice to meet you.'

On her first day at her new school, Karen's heart skipped a beat as she looked around the classroom full of unfamiliar faces.

In the back, she saw a girl who looked like Kana.

That girl was Lutsu Kanamori. Looking back, it wasn't so much her face – it was the quiet dignity in the way she carried herself.

And so, when Ms Suzuta encouraged her – 'Akanishi, the student who transferred out just before you, was in the student council, and we're short on members' – Karen decided to join. Maybe it was because it felt like meeting Kana all over again.

But Lutsu wasn't Kana.

Of course she wasn't. She was a different person. She didn't *need* to be the same. Lutsu had her own wonderful qualities, and the more they got to know each other, the more Karen grew to like her.

Lutsu was more earnest, more dependable and kinder than anyone Karen had met before. She never once frowned when Karen failed her tests, always patiently helping her study.

'You can do it if you try, Karen. I know you can,' she said, wholeheartedly encouraging her.

Karen had never wanted to study before – it had never seemed necessary. But discovering something she didn't know gave her a previously unknown kind of joy.

'I had no idea studying could be this much fun. You'd make a good teacher, Lutsu,' Karen told her one evening as the light of the setting sun filled the student council room.

'. . . Really?' Lutsu asked back, looking genuinely pleased.

'Yeah,' Karen nodded firmly.

'I'm glad . . . The truth is, I've been thinking I'd like to be a teacher.'

It was such a noble dream that Karen – who saw herself as an idiot – felt she could never have come up with it herself.

'That's amazing, Lutsu. You'd be a wonderful teacher!'

Karen took Lutsu's hand, imagining her standing at the front of a classroom. Just as she had once taken Kana's hand. Lutsu's was different – cooler to the touch.

'Thank you, Karen . . . I want to create a classroom free from bullying,' Lutsu said shyly.

In that moment, Karen felt her heart rate spike. 'Free from bullying . . .?' she asked nervously.

'Yeah . . . Just thinking about it makes me sick, but I was bullied myself, back in middle school. It didn't last long, but it was terrifying. I honestly thought about killing myself. I don't want anyone else to have to go through that kind of pain. And if a student ever does, I want to save them.' Lutsu smiled softly in the light of the setting sun.

'. . . You can do it, Lutsu. I mean that.'

Thinking of Kana, and feeling that old pain rise again, Karen gripped Lutsu's hand tighter.

Inside, however, she couldn't shake a strange unease.

If Lutsu dreamed of creating a classroom free from bullying, then why, during gym class, did she never pair up with Mishin?

'Lutsu, do you mind if I pair with Mizushima today in gym?'

The first time Karen asked, Lutsu was visibly startled.

'I just feel bad that she's always paired with Mr Akiyama.' Feeling her chest tighten, Karen offered a suggestion. 'If I partner with her, you could go with the teacher instead – but if you'd rather, I can switch.'

'I don't think Mizushima likes me very much, so it's better if you do . . . I think she'll be really happy.'

'I see . . . Okay, then.'

Karen realized there must have been something between them,

but she didn't press. Everyone had questions they didn't want asked. She had plenty of things she would prefer to keep hidden herself.

'Want to pair up with me, Mizushima?'

When she asked, Mishin looked startled – then, as if she were about to cry.

At their school, bullying meant that Mishin didn't belong to any group at all – that she was treated like a ghost, invisible.

But it wasn't *only* that – not to her. Karen saw it in her face.

'. . . Are you sure?' Mishin asked in a trembling voice.

'Yep!' Karen nodded, taking her hand without further delay.

She didn't know Mishin well – not then, not even now – but she could feel her gentleness in that touch.

Maybe pairing up with Mishin once every couple of weeks was a kind of atonement for Karen. But more than anything, she wished what happened to Kana would never be forced on anyone again – that Mishin wouldn't lose hope to invisible cruelty.

The storm surrounding the classroom had passed, and sunlight began to pour through the windows – perfect for graduation day.

'You understand now, don't you? I don't deserve to live,' Karen muttered, forcing a bitter smile.

Lutsu bowed her head, her expression solemn.

'. . . Still,' Mishin said, 'I was happy. When you paired with me. And today, when everyone joined hands . . . I was happy then, too.'

If Karen wasn't mistaken, Mishin was smiling.

As the game progressed, everyone had wanted to be her partner.

The notion they'd all had that such a sight was impossible had been mistaken all along.

Even when the game started, even when Aria Urushibara was the first to be eliminated, she hadn't felt afraid. Each time someone died, it had felt like just punishment. Even when Nichika died, just moments ago.

People died because of bullying, whether it happened in the open or behind closed doors.

Even if you didn't take part, even if you just looked away, that alone was enough. It was already a death sentence.

'Thank you, Mizushima . . . But I really do think I deserve to die,' Karen Asakura sentenced herself.

'. . . You're wrong,' Mishin said firmly. 'Kana wouldn't have wanted you to die. I can tell. Because even after hearing everything, I still want you to live – you and Lutsu.'

Hearing Mishin call Lutsu by her first name, Karen remembered what had just happened. Lutsu had done the same thing – *Karen, hold hands with Mishin*, she had said.

At that moment, Karen was one hundred per cent sure – there was *definitely* something between them.

'. . . Lutsu and I can't be partners anymore,' she said in a soft murmur. 'Which means you're the only one who can survive, Mizushima. Besides, that's what I've wanted from the start.'

Karen planned to hold Lutsu's hand again and die together. That way, Mishin would be left over, and only she would live. If the pattern held, any two who died together would die peacefully.

But Mishin pointed to the blackboard. 'The rules say, *The last one or two remaining will be permitted to graduate.* So maybe we don't have to be paired.'

Karen's breath caught. She read the rule again. She had been so desperate to pair up with someone during the course of the game that she had completely missed that possibility.

Mishin had spent more time waiting than anyone else, so she must have memorized every rule.

If pairing wasn't required, then maybe Lutsu and Mishin could both survive.

'But it says that if someone's left over, everyone except the designated student is disqualified,' Karen pointed out.

Everyone had been aware of that rule from the start – and it was obvious now that Mishin was indeed the *designated student*.

'No one has to be left over,' Mishin said, her voice steady as she turned her back to her. 'Karen . . . Do you remember the meaning of the snowdrop flower?'

Karen didn't yet understand where that question was leading.

'. . . *I wish for your death,*' she answered, startled that Mishin had called her by her first name.

Mishin nodded. 'I'm really glad I met both of you.'

With that, she began walking toward the classroom door.

Even someone as stupid as Karen understood what she meant to do.

'. . . Mishin, wait!'

Without thinking, she chased after her and grabbed her thin arm. Her heart was pounding so hard she could barely breathe.

But it wasn't she who had moved – it was Lutsu.

Survey on Bullying

This survey is being conducted so that all students can enjoy a positive, enriching school life. Your answers here will not be made public, and you don't have to write your name if you don't want to.

1. Do you feel that bullying is taking place at this school?

   ~~Yes / No~~ *I don't know.*

2. Do you feel that you are being bullied right now?

   Yes / No

3. If you answered 'Yes', what form does the bullying take?

4. Do you feel that you are bullying someone right now, or that you have bullied someone in the past?

   ~~Yes / No~~ *I didn't realize it.*

5. If you answered 'Yes', what form does the bullying take?

   Badmouthing someone in a LINE group.

6. What are your thoughts on bullying?

   I think people who bully others should be sentenced to death.

7. What do you think could be done to eliminate bullying?

   I wish we had a system that imposed the death penalty on those involved in bullying or people who turn a blind eye to it.

Round 15

Karen Asakura - Lutsu Kanamori
Lisa Okami - Mishin Mizushima

<u>Disqualified:</u>
Nichika Saeki
Lisa Okami

<u>Students Remaining:</u> 3

<u>Time Left:</u>
5 minutes

Chapter 16: Congratulations on Graduating
Lutsu Kanamori

'I'm sorry, Mishin . . . I'm so sorry.'

Clinging to her arm – just skin and bone – Lutsu bowed her head. Drops of emotion spilled like beads onto the bloodstained floor. She couldn't bring herself to look at her face. Instead, she watched her tears fall straight down, glimmering clear as glass, and spoke again.

'I'm sorry . . . *I'm* the one who needs to atone. *I'm* the one who deserves the death penalty.'

'Lutsu, hold your head up,' urged Karen Asakura, her voice calm, almost detached. 'Tell me everything. About you two.'

Maybe she had already realized it. No – she *had* realized it.

For someone who had gone on about wanting to make a classroom free from bullying, it must have struck Karen as strange that Lutsu herself had stubbornly refused to partner with Mishin during gym class.

Lutsu nodded, wiped her tears with the back of her hand, and steadied her breathing. Then, she opened her mouth, giving voice to words that had remained unspoken for so long.

'. . . Back in middle school, Mishin and I were best friends.'

Best friends.

'Gym's next, Mishin. Come on, let's go and get changed!'

'Right!'

At school, the two of them were always together. Like magnets that couldn't stay apart, their hands were always linked. There wasn't a single day they didn't share each other's warmth.

*

'Thank you, Kanamori.'

It had been around two months after the school year started – right in the middle of the rainy season – when Mishin first spoke to her.

Lutsu tilted her head. 'Uh . . . Thanks for what?'

'You change the water in the vase sometimes, don't you?' Mishin said, pointing toward the container on the shelf at the back of the classroom.

'Oh, you noticed that?'

'Of course. The flowers in that vase – I grew them myself in the flowerbed out in the courtyard.'

'Right, you're in the gardening club. Thanks for always bringing such pretty flowers.'

'It's nothing. I just thought having flowers in the classroom made it feel nice. But you know, no one really pays attention. I was really happy when I found out you were changing the water.'

Lutsu could still remember the shy smile Mishin gave her at the time.

Back then, Mishin hadn't been treated as the class ghost. Far from it – she was the kind of person who would walk right up to you and start talking. She wasn't especially flashy or beautiful, but she always had people around her.

Lutsu knew it was the overwhelming kindness in Mishin's heart that drew people in.

And in fact, Lutsu had never once heard Mishin gossip about anyone.

In a world where a group of teenage girls almost *couldn't* talk without putting someone down, Lutsu herself had sometimes gone along, nodding at the right times. But Mishin never did.

'Um . . . Mishin? If you're free, do you want to go try the new Starbucks drink?'

That afternoon after school, Lutsu mustered up the courage to walk over to Mishin's desk and talk to her.

Lutsu was the kind of student known only for being a model pupil, while Mishin, who got along with nearly everyone, shone in a way she never could.

'... The new Starbucks drink?' Mishin repeated, tilting her head in confusion.

'Um... To, you know... become friends?' Her voice wavered, but she got the words out.

Lutsu had never really had someone she could call a true friend. Or rather, she had never wanted anyone to be more than a classmate – until Mishin. From the start of the school year, she had felt that they were somehow alike – that they shared the same kind of heart.

And from what she had seen on her classmates' social media posts, going to try the new Starbucks drink together seemed like the first test of friendship.

'Sure, let's go,' Mishin laughed softly and held out her hand.

They sat side by side on the bank of the Kamo River, sipping the new seasonal Strawberry Cheesecake Frappuccino.

'It's *so* sweet.'

'Yeah, *so* sweet.'

Lutsu had never ordered a seasonal special before. She always stuck to her usual caramel macchiato – safe, familiar, predictable. But that day, the sweetness felt different. Maybe because she was with Mishin, it tasted even better.

'So, why did you join the gardening club? I mean... it's not really the most popular one,' Lutsu asked, letting the sugary flavour linger on her tongue.

'Yeah, it's not. It's pretty plain. But I love flowers, so I enjoy it.'

'Why do you love them?'

To be honest, Lutsu didn't really get what was so great about flowers. That spring, when her father had taken her to Maruyama Park to see the cherry blossoms lit up at night, the cold had bothered her more than the beauty. She had just wanted to eat takoyaki and go home.

'Because they're beautiful,' Mishin said while gazing out at the shimmering Kamo River, her eyes cool and clear.

It was such a pure answer – she loved them because they were beautiful. Just like that, Lutsu realized she loved Mishin's honesty, her refusal to speak ill of anyone, her beauty of heart.

They talked about everything until the sun went down, like they had been promising to come to the riverbank together for ages.

By the time they finished their drinks, they were firm friends.

By the next spring, their friendship had deepened enough to call each other *best friends*.

'My mum's on a trip with her friends tonight, so I'll be home alone. Want to come sleep over?'

Mishin only ever invited her when her mother wasn't home.

Her family was just the two of them, and Lutsu had figured out from the look of the place that her mum worked in the nightlife business. Mishin didn't try to hide it.

'Yeah, I'll come.'

They brought snacks from the convenience store, and the nights they spent together, just the two of them, felt different from school. Too excited to sleep, they always ended up talking until morning. Even though they saw each other every day, they somehow never ran out of things to talk about.

Lutsu's home was the opposite – a single-father household. Her father had always been quiet, but after her mother died from illness when Lutsu was nine, he had grown even more withdrawn, throwing himself into work and house chores like a man trying to drown his grief. By the time Lutsu was in her second year of middle school, he had started spending more nights away on what he told her were business trips. As such, it wasn't a big deal if she suddenly stayed over at Mishin's place.

'My dad thinks he's hiding it, but I'm pretty sure he's got a girlfriend now. Guess he's forgotten about Mum. They were so close . . . It kind of hurts,' Lutsu admitted just before dawn.

It had been five years since her mother's death. Her father was still young – barely forty – and Lutsu understood that it was natural for him to want to start a new life. Everyone needed someone, especially when they were lonely. He was smiling more these days, too.

'Yeah . . . That's really sad.'

Even when her heart was heavy, Mishin's gentle nod always seemed to lift some of the weight away, like magic.

'Do you think there's such a thing as feelings that never change?' Lutsu asked. She wanted to believe there was.

'Well, my feelings for *you* will never change.'

Outside, the sky was turning white – the space between night and morning reflected in Mishin's eyes as she smiled at her.

'Yeah. Mine won't ever change, either,' Lutsu replied.

She could still remember the warmth of their hands, naturally finding each other under the blankets.

'When I'm with you, Mishin, I feel like I can really be myself.' Lutsu squeezed her hand tightly.

'Me too.'

They didn't need to say *Let's be best friends forever*. It was obvious. Their bond would never change. Lutsu believed that completely. And she was sure Mishin did, as well.

But their *forever* ended just three months later.

It began when one of the seven girls in the top clique – the group that included Sae, the leader, and Katsune Nakano – was suddenly sidelined.

Rumour had it the girl had been seen walking with the guy Sae was dating from another school.

'Um . . . I don't think it's right to ignore someone or leave them out like that,' Lutsu said to Sae about a week into it.

The other girls in the group glared at her.

Sae blinked, then smiled that frighteningly perfect smile that only the top girls could pull off. 'You're right. I'll be careful.'

Lutsu felt a chill, but also breathed a sigh of relief. As the class representative, she thought it was her duty to deal with any problems between students. She truly believed that no matter how small the bullying, if they talked it through, they would come to understand each other.

The next day, the girl who had been ostracized was back with the group as if nothing had happened. Lutsu was proud of herself for speaking up. But that sense of accomplishment lasted only until lunch.

Because in exchange, there were bugs in Lutsu's lunchbox.

As she let out a shriek, Katsune and the others snickered from across the room.

Lutsu quickly shut the lid and threw away the homemade lunch she had packed in a cheap one-hundred-yen store box. She didn't have the courage to open it again.

'Lutsu, are you okay? Whoever did that is awful. Eat with me instead,' Mishin offered.

But Lutsu had lost her appetite. Realizing this wasn't going to stop today, she promised herself she would just buy bread from now on.

That night, a notification from the class LINE group proved her right.

'You know what real bullying is?'

The message came from Sae's account, and it was clearly meant for her.

What followed – the *real bullying* – was too cruel for a fourteen-year-old to endure. There were days when simple silence felt like heaven compared to everything else.

The worst was being locked inside the cleaning-supply closet.

When she was little, Lutsu had hidden in a wardrobe during hide-and-seek and gotten trapped for half a day. Ever since, she had been terrified of dark, closed spaces. She panicked, pounding the door until her fists hurt, but no matter how much she screamed, no one would let her out unless a teacher happened to be walking by.

After a month of that, Lutsu's heart was so shredded that she couldn't think of anything but wanting to die. Each time she was hit by someone's malice, she realized just how fragile her faith in justice really was.

Her only hope left was Mishin. Without her, Lutsu might actually have gone through with it.

In that classroom, Mishin was the only person who gave her a place to belong.

'Let's be partners,' Mishin said during gym class, the same as always.

She never retreated to the safety of the majority. She remained Lutsu's friend.

And because of that – because she stayed – the target shifted.

The very next day, after Mishin rescued Lutsu from the locker and screamed, 'Bullying is so childish!' across the classroom, the arrows turned toward her instead.

'Hey, Lutsu, let's be partners.'

That day in gym class, Katsune came up to her, probably under Sae's orders, and called out to her as if they were close friends.

Lutsu knew right away what it meant. That was the signal, the sign that the bullying was over.

And at the same time, she understood that if she took Katsune's hand, all that malice that had been aimed at her would shift to Mishin.

'Yeah.'

But she couldn't refuse. She was scared – terrified. The mere thought of going against them and returning to those days of torment made her feel like she was going to faint.

After that, when the target changed from her to Mishin, the bullying became worse – so much worse that she couldn't even bear to look at it.

There was a very simple reason for that – because Lutsu hadn't stood up for Mishin.

And because of it, every time the teacher said, 'Get into pairs,' Mishin always ended up alone.

About a month after she had taken Katsune's hand, Lutsu got a LINE message from Mishin: *'Want to go try the new Starbucks drink after school?'*

'Sure,' Lutsu replied right away, relieved.

Ever since that day, she hadn't been able to talk to Mishin at school. She had been too afraid Mishin might hate her, too afraid to message her first. The truth was, she had wanted to apologize every single day – for letting her inadequate sense of justice lead to all of this, for being too afraid to help.

She thought maybe, outside of school, she could finally talk to her properly.

'Um, Mishin . . . I –'

But just as she started to confess, sitting with Mishin by the Kamo River where they had first talked alone –

'Let's not hang out anymore, Lutsu.'

That was what Mishin said.

'. . . Not hang out?'

A sharp pain shot through her chest. The Strawberry Delight Frappuccino she had just bought slipped from her hand, spilling over. Pink cream and whipped topping trickled into the Kamo River.

As she watched it flow away, Mishin went on. 'Yeah. Let's stop talking. Completely.'

Her tone wasn't angry, but it was clear there was no taking that back.

'Mishin . . . I – I –'

Lutsu grabbed her hand without thinking.

She wanted to apologize, but before the words could come, tears overflowed and choked her voice.

'Don't cry, Lutsu. I'll be fine,' Mishin said with the faintest of smiles.

Even through her tears, Lutsu could tell it was a sad smile.

'Hey, Lutsu, even if we stop talking to each other, let's still be best friends, okay? That feeling won't ever change.'

Mishin's warm hand gently squeezed her own cold fingers.

Lutsu couldn't say a thing. It took all she had just to nod again and again, gripping that hand tightly through her tears.

The next-to-last time they had had to pair up in a game – that was the last time Lutsu ever held Mishin's hand.

'Mishin . . . I'm sorry . . . I'm *so* sorry. This is all my fault. Everything.'

Lutsu was sobbing uncontrollably. She knew she had no right to cry. Back then, it was Mishin who had had every reason to cry.

'. . . You know, I was really happy when you paired up with me,' Mishin said.

She spoke the same way she used to when they were friends – like nothing had changed since those days by the river.

'I'd always been hoping for that. That someday, you'd take my hand again.'

At that sad smile, every feeling Lutsu had been holding back surged up inside her.

After Mishin had cut her off, Lutsu had mustered the courage to send her a LINE message. But it never went through – Mishin had probably blocked her. So, on graduation day at middle school, Lutsu had planned to congratulate her in person. Maybe then they could start over.

That was the only reason she had gone to this low-ranked high school – to be with Mishin again.

But Mishin never came to the graduation ceremony.

And once high school started, she couldn't bring herself to be Mishin's friend again.

Because Katsune was in the same class.

Despite all her studying, Katsune had failed her first-choice school. And in front of someone who knew everything, Lutsu couldn't just walk up to Mishin like nothing had happened. The fear of having the past exposed – and the bullying start all over – kept her silent.

More than anything, it felt natural to assume Mishin didn't think of her as a friend anymore – that she probably hated her enough to want her dead.

'. . . I always kind of knew you two were friends,' Karen murmured when Lutsu's tears got the better of her. 'I'd seen you sometimes, looking at the flowerbeds in the courtyard in the mornings. And even after this game started, you were always worried about Mishin, weren't you?'

Lutsu wiped her eyes on her sleeve and nodded slowly.

Yes. She had gone to see the flowers Mishin had grown to remind herself – and to punish herself. She wanted forgiveness for betraying her, for lacking the courage to pair up again. And she wanted to atone.

That was why, when this game started, she hadn't paired with Karen in the first round. It hadn't been about surviving together. It had been part of her plan – to let Mishin and Karen survive.

Cruel as it sounded, if it looked like Mishin would be left out in that first round, she had intended to betray one of the twins and take Mishin's hand herself.

She had urged everyone to focus on the *designated student*, and she had rigged the vote by saying, *Please raise your hand if you vote for Mizushima*. All of it was to make Mishin sit out safely – to make sure those two would live.

'You really are smart, Karen.' Lutsu sniffled, giving her a faint smile. 'When you showed up in the student council room that day, it felt like a new life had started for me. When I told you I wanted to become a teacher and make a classroom free from bullying, and you said, *You can do it, Lutsu*. Those words brought light into my hopeless heart. The time we spent together after school – it made me feel like I was myself again, before all the bullying. I'm proud to have been your friend.'

Karen nodded along. Lutsu could feel a flower coming to

life inside her battered heart – a flower as beautiful as the ones Mishin grew.

'Like I said, Karen, you're smart. You're definitely not stupid. You learned fast – every problem I explained, you got it right away . . . And you weren't afraid. You faced your past and acted. You paired up with Mishin. I couldn't do anything but protect myself. That's why I think you're amazing. Really.'

As she finished, Lutsu thought – yes, Karen was the one who deserved to survive.

'Thanks, Lutsu. You know, I had so much fun being with you, too. It helped me not think about Kana's death. It even felt like I was talking to her again. I got into college thanks to you, and for the first time, I feel confident in myself. If we hadn't become friends, I think I'd still be stuck, unable to do anything. I'm sure of it – you'll be a great teacher someday.'

Karen smiled, then turned toward Mishin.

'Hey, Mizushima. Your dream is to open a flower shop someday, right? I can already picture it – everyone coming to buy the flowers you've grown with so much love. I don't really have a dream myself, so I want you two to survive . . . Besides, you'll always be best friends, right?'

As she spoke, Karen pressed her hand against the corsage at her breast. Lutsu's chest tightened – Karen was all but saying she was about to end her own life.

Lutsu rushed forward, grabbed her arm, and screamed, 'Please form pairs!'

- Please form pairs.

That was the very first rule on the blackboard.

'. . . If you don't form a pair, you're disqualified. The part about one or two people – that's only for when someone gets left out. If two people are going to survive, they have to be partners.'

From the moment she and Karen paired up – or rather, she and Mishin – Lutsu had understood that the only surviving combination could be Mishin and Karen. She herself would be disqualified.

She took a deep breath, still holding Karen's arm, and turned to Mishin. 'I'm so sorry . . . I know this isn't something I can be forgiven for. But please, believe me about this one thing. What Karen asked earlier . . . I still think of you as my best friend. That feeling has never changed.'

And that was true – because Mishin had always been on her side. If not for this game, she might never have had the courage to take her hand again.

'But I betrayed you, Mishin. I didn't pair with you. Your feelings must have changed since that day . . . right?'

Mishin's cool eyes, half-hidden by her bangs, locked on her.

Yet she said nothing. That silence was her answer.

'Mishin, Karen – thank you for being my friends.'

Lutsu smiled at them both. She knew it must have been a sad smile.

Sunlight broke through the clouds, shining at their feet.

One minute remaining.

Without hesitation, Lutsu took Mishin's wrist and brought her hand toward Karen's, like pulling two magnets together.

And Mishin gently took Karen's hand.

'Congratulations on graduating,' Lutsu said, holding back her tears.

She had decided, from the very start of this game, that those would be her last words.

Survey on Bullying

This survey is being conducted so that all students can enjoy a positive, enriching school life. Your answers here will not be made public, and you don't have to write your name if you don't want to.

1. Do you feel that bullying is taking place at this school?

[Yes] / No

2. Do you feel that you are being bullied right now?

   Yes / [No]

3. If you answered 'Yes', what form does the bullying take?

   For example, when the teacher says 'Form pairs' during gym class, and a certain student always ends up left out.

4. Do you feel that you are bullying someone right now, or that you have bullied someone in the past?

   [Yes] / No

5. If you answered 'Yes', what form does the bullying take?

   I didn't take that certain student's hand.

6. What are your thoughts on bullying?

   I don't think it's something that can ever be forgiven. It's something that should disappear completely.

7. What do you think could be done to eliminate bullying?

   Unless you've been bullied yourself, you can't really understand how painful it is. But being on the bullied side means losing every last bit of hope. In that darkness, you can't see anything at all. Some people, out of that fear, end up losing their dearest friends, or even their own lives. And that's something you can never take back. It's even sadder than the bullying itself. That's why I want to become a teacher someday, and create a classroom free from bullying.

Round 16

Graduates:
Karen Asakura
Mishin Mizushima

Disqualified:
Lutsu Kanamori

Time Left:
1 minute

Chapter 17: Designated Student
Mishin Mizushima

'The graduation ceremony is about to begin. Graduating students, please leave your classrooms and proceed to the auditorium.'

As the petals began to scatter from Lutsu Kanamori's uniform, an announcement crackled from the yellowed speaker above the blackboard. It was Ms Suzuta's voice, which Mishin felt like she hadn't heard in forever.

'Don't worry about me. Go,' Lutsu said, voice trembling.

But just like Karen Asakura, Mishin couldn't make herself move.

The thought of leaving Lutsu alone to die in a classroom littered with the bodies of the twenty-four students who had already been disqualified was unbearable. Lutsu must have been terrified inside, no matter how calm she tried to pretend she was.

'. . . You'll get disqualified. Hurry!' Lutsu shouted, pointing at the clock.

- The last one or two remaining will be permitted to graduate. Graduates must not be late to the ceremony.

There was less than a minute left until the 10:00 deadline.

'. . . Let's go,' Karen said, squeezing Mishin's hand tight.

Mishin understood then – she had made up her mind. She wanted to make sure Lutsu's death wasn't in vain.

Mishin squeezed her hand back and nodded.

The classroom was on the second floor, and the gymnasium – the auditorium – was just downstairs. If they ran with everything they had, they could make it.

Leaving Lutsu behind, the two of them burst out of the classroom like they were taking flight.

The explosion came barely ten seconds later.

Karen stopped for an instant, but she didn't turn back. Neither did Mishin. They didn't have the time or the courage to look. They didn't need to think about it – they both knew what that sound meant.

Maybe once they had joined hands, they were already recognized as a pair. Maybe it wouldn't have mattered if they let go. But they didn't. They kept running, gripping each other so tightly their palms hurt.

The last time Mishin had run this hard was back in her first year of middle school, during the sports festival – back when she and Lutsu had just become friends.

They made it to the gym right before the time limit.

There weren't any chairs, no red-and-white banners – nothing that said *Graduation Ceremony*. It was the same drab gym as always, just emptier somehow.

No teachers, no sound – only Karen's quiet sobs echoing through the stillness.

They had been running for their lives, so Mishin hadn't even realized Karen was crying until they stopped.

'Congratulations on graduating.'

The voice came from the stage. It was Ms Suzuta.

Mishin steadied her breath and looked up.

Now that the game was over, there were so many things she wanted to ask. But she knew there was no point. Karen must have felt the same. Without wiping away her tears, she stared at their homeroom teacher in silence.

'So, this time . . . you two ended up as a pair.' Ms Suzuta's voice was low, shadowed, as she looked down at them.

This time.

. . . Which meant no one had paired up last time?

She had said before the game began that this wasn't the first *special lesson*.

But come to think of it, Sarasa Hoshikawa had been right. If an entire class of students had died, it would have been a national scandal. And yet, Mishin had never heard of such a horrific murder game in the news.

Ms Suzuta must have guessed her thoughts.

'. . . Do you two know about the bus accident seven years ago?' she asked. 'The one in Nagano, where a tour bus carrying students on a graduation trip fell off a cliff and everyone on board died?'

Seven years ago . . . Mishin would have been in fifth grade. Her mother worked nights, so she had spent her evenings watching TV alone. She could vaguely remember seeing the reports.

'The news said the surviving student was absent from the trip because of illness, but that wasn't the truth. The game happened inside that moving bus – and I was the only one who survived. Because at the end, I didn't take anyone's hand. No one was my friend. Or to put it another way, no one ever wanted to *be* my friend. So, when everyone started dying . . . I was glad. I was thrilled, watching them all suddenly beg to hold my hand. They'd always treated me like a ghost, ignored me, and then – when they realized they might die – they called my name, acted like we'd been close, clinging to me. It was pathetic. It was *hilarious*.' Ms Suzuta smiled faintly, no doubt reminiscing on her own *graduation game*.

It was the same kind of smile Mishin had once given Lutsu – one so full of pain it almost hurt to look at.

'I became a teacher because I wanted to be like the woman who saved me through that special lesson. Thanks to that game, I learned to have hope in life. I came to believe that people who kill others' hearts will face punishment. And I decided that if I ever had a student like me, I'd save them. Because I know that even invisible bullying can feel like a loneliness so deep it makes you want to die . . . I thought that the designated student would be glad the game was happening, just like I once was. So . . . why are you crying, Mishin Mizushima?'

Startled by her question, Mishin came back to herself.

Just like Karen with her tears, she hadn't even realized she was crying.

Maybe she had been crying ever since the day she told Lutsu they shouldn't talk to each other anymore.

'. . . Because I *had* a best friend,' she answered as the warmth of her tears trickled down her cheeks.

She remembered it clearly. That day when she had said goodbye, it hadn't been out of anger. It was because she didn't want the bullying to shift back to Lutsu. She didn't want to see her get hurt again. Lutsu had been important to her.

Those feelings hadn't changed. Or at least, she thought they hadn't.

But when Lutsu had asked her earlier if they were still the same, Mishin hadn't been able to answer.

Even though she had accepted being the new target, she couldn't bring herself to say Lutsu was still her best friend – not after she had let her suffer without ever helping, not after she had taken Katsune's hand without hesitation and never once paired with her again.

A short silence stretched out between the three of them, when all of a sudden, the shrill sound of the fire alarm blared throughout the school.

The piercing noise made Mishin's head spin. She looked around, but there was no sign of fire inside the gymnasium.

'Don't worry,' Ms Suzuta said coolly. 'This place won't burn. Not yet.'

The way she said it made it clear she herself had started the fire somewhere else on the campus grounds.

'This game, and this school, will all be erased in flames. *You* were the designated student, Mizushima, the one meant to survive. Because you had no friends. You were supposed to go straight home after the ceremony. You would certainly have no reason to stay behind and take pictures with your classmates . . . That was what I was going to have you testify to the police. But that's impossible now. Because you, Karen Asakura, survived as well.'

She was no longer trying to hide the hatred in her voice.

Mishin realized then that Ms Suzuta knew why Karen had changed schools.

That was why she handed out the bullying survey just after Karen joined the class – and why she had lied saying it was being distributed nationwide.

Mishin had been curious afterward. She had searched online to see if other schools had gotten the same survey, but there hadn't been a single mention of it. Not on social media, not in any forum. Despite supposedly being sent to every school in the country.

It had been too strange. That was when Mishin had understood – though she never imagined it was for this *game* – that Ms Suzuta had made it for her.

'During gym, you were the only one who paired up with Mizushima. Whatever your past may be, I respected you for that. Even if it came from guilt, to Mizushima, you must have seemed like a god. If someone like you had reached out to me back when I was a student, maybe I would have wanted to survive with them, too.' Ms Suzuta paused, then asked softly, 'Tell me, Mizushima – if the last one left hadn't been Asakura, would you have been able to pair up with them?'

It was the first time in three years that Mishin felt as though her teacher was accusing her of wrongdoing. But even now, with everything that had happened, she couldn't bring herself to hate her.

'No,' Mishin said quietly.

And she meant it.

If the last one standing hadn't been Karen, she probably wouldn't have taken anyone's hand, either – just like Ms Suzuta.

'Um . . .'

At that moment –

'What happened to the parents and the other teachers?' Karen's voice cut sharply through the air.

Startled, Mishin suddenly remembered – her mother was supposed to come to the ceremony today.

'The other teachers have been in the basement storage room since yesterday. Bullying is something enabled by schools, so they have to take responsibility.'

That could only mean she had locked them in. The basement

was deep underground. There was no mobile signal down there, and the heavy door couldn't be opened from the inside. And it wouldn't raise any alarms if an adult, especially one in a demanding job like a teacher, didn't come back for a day. Someone like Ms Suzuta, who could design a game this elaborate, could easily falsify any messages needed to cover her tracks.

'I couldn't get the decorations out, so it's a rather plain affair. I'm sorry about that. As for the parents, I told them the ceremony would start at eleven, so they won't get caught in the fire. You can relax.'

Instead of feeling relieved, Mishin found herself impressed. It was true – no student actually read the notes sent home to parents. A month ago, she had forwarded it to her mum without even checking the contents.

'What about you, Ms Suzuta?' Karen asked next.

'Of course, I'll take full responsibility for my part. That rule has been in place from the beginning,' she said, her faint smile shrouded in shadow.

There hadn't been any such rule written on the blackboard, but the blaring fire alarm made it hard for Mishin to think about that now.

Then came a sharp crash – the sound of shattering glass. The flames were already closing in. Once they spread, it would only be a matter of time before this small school building, the oldest in all of Kyoto, was razed to the ground.

'Let's go, Mishin,' Karen said firmly.

It was the first time she had ever called Mishin by her first name.

'Yeah,' Mishin nodded, unable to calm her racing heart.

Leaving their homeroom teacher behind, the two of them ran out of the gymnasium.

Through the hallway, under the arched front entrance, and outside, where the sky was a stretch of pure blue. The storm from earlier was gone as if it had never been, a soft spring breeze blowing across the school grounds.

Carried by that breeze, Mishin ran, her hand in Karen's.

*

After crossing the street and passing through Yasaka Shrine, they finally arrived at Maruyama Park.

'Let's sit over there.' Catching her breath, Karen pointed toward a stone bench by the pond.

Mishin nodded, struggling to steady her breathing.

Ever since pairing up at the end, they hadn't let go of each other's hands once. Mishin was too afraid to, and Karen must have felt the same, because even after they sat down, their hands remained clasped.

The park's famous weeping cherry trees had just begun to bloom, a few soft petals showing here and there.

'. . . What Yayoi said about the cherry blossoms waiting for their friends – it was a lovely story,' Karen murmured as she stared at the blossoms.

Mishin remembered it, too. Yayoi Yoitani had talked about it right before she was disqualified – that the first cherry blossom to bloom would wait, refusing to scatter until the very last bud had opened.

'Yeah.'

A flock of pigeons circled lazily around the tree.

Mishin couldn't quite believe she was still alive. The death game that they had been thrown into so suddenly was over. Her classmates had been killed one after another, and yet somehow, she and Karen had survived. It felt so unreal – like she had just woken from a dream.

'I wish it *had* all just been a dream . . .' Karen whispered as if reading her mind.

For her, Lutsu – her best friend – had died, and she had survived with someone who wasn't a friend. To her, this must have felt like a nightmare.

'. . . I'm sorry.'

The words slipped out before Mishin could stop them, her gaze falling to the ground. There was no way she couldn't feel responsible. That *special lesson* had been meant to punish students who had bullied others out of unconscious malice. In other words, the game had happened because of her – because *she* had been the *designated student*. And her classmates had died because of it.

'Why are you apologizing?'

'Because . . . I killed Lutsu.'

She had taken Karen's hand – the one Lutsu had pulled toward her at the very end. It was that action that had sealed Lutsu's fate. And yet, at that moment, Mishin hadn't felt so much as a trace of doubt.

'Why would you think that?'

'. . . Do you remember, a year ago, when we talked about the meaning of snowdrops?'

Karen nodded slightly.

'That time, when you asked me if there was anyone I wished would die . . . Lutsu's face came to mind.' Mishin's voice quivered. 'I was shocked at myself for thinking that. I didn't want to believe it. But if, just now, Lutsu had been the last one left alive . . . I don't think I could have taken her hand. Even when she was disqualified, there was a part of me that couldn't really grieve . . . If anything, I almost felt like all those painful days I wanted to die were somehow finally justified . . . And I realized something during the game – these three years, Lutsu never once paired with me again. Somewhere along the way, I had come to hate her so much that I wanted her gone. I hadn't even realized it until the game brought it all out . . .'

The bullying had kindled a terrible, helpless malice inside of her.

What had hurt the most wasn't when they had put bugs in her lunch. It was when her best friend Lutsu kept ignoring her.

Even after Mishin had cut ties with Lutsu to keep her from getting dragged into more cruelty, she had believed, all the way up to graduation, that her best friend would reach out again someday.

'Hey, Mishin . . . Lutsu wanted to be a teacher one day. She dreamed of leading a classroom free from bullying. That was because she regretted not being able to protect you. So, no matter how you felt, I think she was happy that, through this game, she got to protect her best friend,' Karen said without any hint of blame. 'And even if this game had happened at my old school, and if I'd made it to the end, and if Kana hadn't paired with me, I still wouldn't have thought she killed me. Because I was the one who failed her.'

When Karen confessed her sins near the end of the game, Mishin had understood exactly how she felt – and the despair that Kana must have felt, too. She also understood how Ms Suzuta, who had been treated like a ghost by her high school class just like she had, must have felt saved by this twisted lesson.

No matter the time or the place, there would always be students living on the edge of despair, unable to find hope.

After a short silence, Mishin took a deep breath. 'Snowdrops . . . have another meaning.'

'. . . What is it?' Karen asked, sounding a little frightened.

Mishin lifted her head and looked her straight in the eyes. 'Hope.'

No matter how desperate things seemed, if there was even a single spark of hope, people could still go on living.

Mishin believed that if each student in that suffocating, lonely classroom could find just a single friend, everyone would have been saved.

For her, that person had long been Lutsu – the hope that one day, she might pair with her again. But that changed the day Karen appeared before her, stretching out her hand and saying, 'Want to pair up with me?'

Even through the nightmare of the game, what kept Mishin wanting to live until the end was Karen's presence – the hope that if they survived together, they might become true friends.

'Karen.'

It was only the second time she had said her name out loud.

She had always wanted to call her by her first name, not her last – like a real friend would.

That was why, even when she had been ready to be disqualified, she had wanted to fulfil that wish before dying.

'Thank you . . . for always being my partner.'

As soon as she said it, a flood of emotions broke loose, tears spilling onto the deep blue fabric of her skirt.

'Thank *you*, too – for being mine at the end.' Karen smiled through her own tears.

Mishin had always thought that someone like Karen, at the top of the social ladder, could never understand what it was like to live at the bottom. But she had been wrong. Everyone carried their own sorrow. Even those who had died – there hadn't been a single one of them untouched by sadness.

Lutsu, too – she must have suffered, tormented by the guilt of betraying her best friend. That was why, in the game, she had accepted her death and protected Mishin until the very last moment.

Mishin had never seen her standing by the flowerbeds every morning. She had always come to school late, wanting to spend as little time there as possible. But if she had known back when it might have mattered, maybe everything would have turned out differently.

Now, at last, the weight of Lutsu's death hit her, and all she could was cry.

'You could've told me the nice meaning first,' Karen said half-jokingly as she tried to wipe away her tears.

That was when it happened. She must have lifted her dominant hand without thinking, and their hands, still joined until that moment, slipped apart.

For an instant, tension shot through the air. Karen froze, then met Mishin's eyes and nodded. Before wiping away her tears, she quietly unpinned the corsage from her uniform.

Seconds passed. The horrible reaction that marked the ongoing game never came. It was just a fake flower now.

It really was over.

In the distance, they could hear the wail of fire engines racing toward the burning school.

'Mishin . . . Are you going to tell anyone about what happened?' Karen asked, letting out a tired breath.

Mishin shook her head. With the school on fire, everything would be reduced to ash. No one would believe them. And besides . . . telling people wouldn't bring anyone back.

'Then how about this – let's say we skipped the ceremony. We ditched together, so we weren't caught in the fire. That sound okay?'

It seemed Karen didn't plan to tell anyone, either.

Mishin nodded – and at that moment, she saw someone about ten metres ahead.

There was no mistaking her. It was her mum, standing there blankly, gazing up at the cherry blossoms.

She looked just the same as before, as beautiful as ever.

Mishin had wanted to see her for so long, had dreamed of this moment. Even when she had been bullied – when they had filled her lunchbox with bugs – she had still loved watching her mum wake up early every morning to make lunch for her. She had loved her so much she couldn't bring herself to say she didn't need it anymore.

But now, after these four years, that feeling had changed.

Mishin turned away from her mother before she could notice her and said casually, 'Hey, Karen. If we're skipping anyway . . . want to go try the new drink at Starbucks?'

'Starbucks? Why Starbucks?' Karen repeated, puzzled – just like Mishin herself had once before.

Even if feelings changed, the happiness they had shared would never fade.

Mishin reached toward Karen, smiling like a flower in full bloom. 'To become friends.'

The hand she took had the same warmth as the one she once longed to hold – the hand of the best friend she had paired with so many times before.

Survey on Bullying

This survey is being conducted so that all students can enjoy a positive, enriching school life. Your answers here will not be made public, and you don't have to write your name if you don't want to.

1. Do you feel that bullying is taking place at this school?

   Yes / [No]

2. Do you feel that you are being bullied right now?

   Yes / [No]

3. If you answered 'Yes', what form does the bullying take?

   ____

4. Do you feel that you are bullying someone right now, or that you have bullied someone in the past?

   Yes / [No]

5. If you answered 'Yes', what form does the bullying take?

   ____

6. What are your thoughts on bullying?

   I hope it disappears.

7. What do you think could be done to eliminate bullying?

   For example, in gym class, there shouldn't be students who always end up paired with the teacher. If everyone took turns and got a chance to be partners with each other, maybe that would help.

   No matter what happens, I want to keep holding on to hope.

Epilogue: Panic
The Designated Student

'Oh, morning, Mami.'

'Morning, Asuka.'

'Can you believe it's actually graduation day?'

'For real.'

'Not being able to wear this uniform anymore is going to be, like, a nightmare.'

'Right?'

'But hey, look – these corsages are kinda cute, aren't they?'

'I thought so, too. It's usually roses or something.'

'I wonder what kind of flower this is?'

'No idea.'

'By the way, did you see that death game video that started blowing up yesterday?'

'I did! The one that starts with *Please form pairs*, right? Is that a movie or something? Like one of those old POV horror things?'

'I don't know. But it's super gory.'

'Way too gory. How hasn't it been banned?'

''Cause it's a movie, maybe? Though it totally looks like some amateur made it.'

'The video quality's trash, anyway. You can't even hear half the dialogue, and it just cuts off at the end.'

'Yeah, seriously. What even happens at the end?'

'Oh, and apparently that YouTuber Urin is in it. You know her?'

'Never heard of her. Is she famous?'

'Seems like she used to be.'

'Huh.'

'I looked it up, and apparently, she died seven years ago – in that graduation day school fire in Kyoto.'

'Wait, wasn't that the one where the teacher said she wanted to bring an end to bullying and burned the whole school down?'

'What? That actually happened? That's insane.'

'Yeah. I was still in elementary school, so I don't remember much, but I think like forty people – students and teachers – died.'

'Oh, I think I remember that. Only two students survived, right?'

'Yeah, that's the one. How'd they escape again?'

'Apparently, they skipped the ceremony and were at Starbucks.'

'No way! That's hilarious.'

'But seriously, whoever wrote that on the blackboard totally copied it from the video.'

'It's way too similar to be a coincidence.'

'For real.'

'Hey, who wrote this?'

'No idea.'

'Anyone know?'

'Nope.'

'Eh, whatever. Still, that *Find a partner or die* thing? Way too creepy.'

'Not just creepy – messed up.'

'Oh, by the way, did you watch *Sea*?'

'Yeah, I saw it on Netflix. Emi Akanishi is amazing.'

'Right? It's all about real actors now. Just being cute and acting terrible? Total dealbreaker.'

'You can fix your face with surgery, but bad acting's forever. Though I'm not into those plastic-looking actresses, either.'

'No kidding.'

'But our homeroom teacher? No way that face is surgery. You can tell.'

'Ren-Ren? Yeah, she's flawless. Totally natural.'

'Seriously, why'd she become a teacher? She could've been a celebrity.'

'Actually, now that you mention it . . . That girl in the video, the pretty one – doesn't she kinda look like Ren-Ren?'

'Wait, really?'

'Yeah, totally. I think her name was Karen or something, too.'

'Seriously? There were so many characters, I didn't even remember their names.'

'Oh, speak of the devil.'

'Okay everyone, good morning!'

'Morning, Ren-Ren! You look so cute today! We're stanning for you!'

'Teachers aren't meant to be *stanned*, you know.'

'A-ha-ha!'

'Uh, Ren-Ren? The blackboard – we don't know who wrote all that.'

'Oh, that's fine – *I* wrote it.'

'Wait, what? Seriously?'

'Did you watch the video, too, Ren-Ren?'

'Yes, I did.'

'Don't tell me . . . the girl in it was actually you or something?'

'That's right. I was one of the students in that game. And now, it's your turn to play.'

'Eh?'

'I think most of you have already seen the video, so I'll skip the explanation. Before we begin class, I just want to add one important word.'

Hope.

'That's what the flower you're all wearing on your corsage symbolizes! My best friend's a florist, and she made them especially for today – with the wish that you'd all carry hope within you. Oh, and by the way – if you take it off, you'll be disqualified. So, be careful, okay?'

'. . . Huh? Disqualified?'

'Ren-Ren? What's going on?'

'Disqualified? Like in the video? Don't joke about that, it's creepy.'

'You're such a scaredy-cat, Mami. It's obviously just a prank. Look – it's just a flower.'

'Yeah, exactly.'

'But still . . .'

'Come on, Mami, you're such a wimp. I'll prove it to you. In the video, the second they took the corsage off, they got covered in flowers and died, right? As if.'

'Wait, stop!'

'It's fine, relax –'

'. . . Ah.'

'Aaaaaahhhhhh!'

'Oh dear . . . I literally just said taking off the corsage means disqualification.'

'. . . Ren-Ren? What *was* that just now?'

'Some kind of magic trick?'

'Asuka's completely covered in flowers.'

'It's just like in the video . . .'

'Did Asuka . . . die?'

'Hey, Ren-Ren, seriously – what *is* this? Is this for real?'

'Yes. One hundred per cent real.'

'. . . Hold on. In the video, the death game only happened in classes that had bullying, right? Our class doesn't have any. So why us?'

'Yeah, *we* don't have bullying!'

'Everyone, please, calm down. And you, Ms Asakura – did you hit your head or something? If this is some kind of prank, you know you'll get arrested and executed, right?'

'Good point, class representative. You're right – what I'm doing is punishable by death. But I was supposed to be executed anyway, so don't worry about it. It's embarrassing to admit, but I used to be such an idiot.'

'. . . Huh?'

'Alright then, let's begin our final lesson. Do you all understand that people can die because of bullying? Even the kind of bullying you can't see? That's why anyone who bullies deserves the death penalty. And those who look away are equally guilty. So, today, through this special lesson, I want you all to think about bullying.

Even you – watching on the other side of the screen. Are you really sure that *you've* never bullied anyone?'

'. . . Wait, *other side of the screen*? What?'

'Are we being livestreamed right now . . .?'

'It's live . . . It's actually live!'

'Why?'

'This is freaking me out!'

'I wanna go home . . .'

'Um . . . Excuse me, Ms Asakura, can I ask one question?'

'Of course.'

'If this game really is about to start, then who exactly is the *designated student* mentioned on the board?'

'You already know the answer to that, don't you?'

With those words, everyone turned to look at *me*.

'Alright then – please form pairs!'

About the Author

Chiren Kina began writing in her student years and made her professional debut after winning the R-18 Literature Prize for Women by Women. To date, her novel *Please Form Pairs* has sold over 130,000 copies in print in Japan.

This brazen book was created by:

Publisher: Romilly Morgan
Editorial Director: Ella Gordon
Editor: Scarlet Furness
Assistant Editor: Emily Campbell
Creative Director: Mel Four
Typesetter: Six Red Marbles UK
Production Controller: Sarah Parry
Sales: Lucy Helliwell
Publicity & Marketing: Charlotte Sanders & Rosa Patel